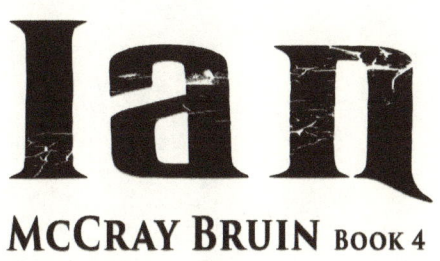

Ian

McCRAY BRUIN BOOK 4

KATHI S. BARTON

This is a work of fiction. Names, characters, places, and incidents are products of the author's imagination or are used fictitiously and are not to be construed as real. Any resemblance to actual events, locations, organizations, or persons, living or dead, is entirely coincidental.

World Castle Publishing, LLC
Pensacola, Florida
Copyright © Kathi S. Barton 2020
Paperback ISBN: 9781953271037
eBook ISBN: 9781953271044
First Edition World Castle Publishing, LLC, August 10, 2020.
http://www.worldcastlepublishing.com
Cover: Karen Fuller
Editor: Maxine Bringenberg

Chapter 1

Ian waited in the lobby for Lucy to be brought back to the ER department. She'd been gone for about an hour when his dad had brought her sisters in, just to have them looked over too, he told him. Jilly sat across from him while Cybill glared at him from several seats away. It was his nature to laugh at someone disliking him. He thought, however, if he did that now, even the hospital wouldn't be able to save him. They'd kill him that quickly.

"What are you?" Ian asked Jilly what she meant. "You're not human. I don't think you are. So, tell me if I'm wrong or what you are. I don't want to be waking up some time with you looming over me like some sort of monster. Not that we're going to be staying with you or anyone else."

"First of all, take it down a notch. I've given you no reason whatsoever to be nasty to me. Also, I'm not going to loom over any of you. I'm a black bear. My entire family is." She glared at him harder. "Look, why don't you just say what you're thinking and we'll go on from there? We've done everything we said we would without once trying to loom or any of the other things going on in your mind."

"What's going to happen to my sister and I when you force Lucy to come and be your slave?" Ian stood up and walked away from her. He wasn't going to lose his temper with a kid. Not today. "Where the hell are you going? I'm speaking to you."

"No, you're not. Speaking to me would mean you're having a conversation with me. All you've done since you were brought here was snip and snap at me like I was the one that left you at the side of the road. I'd never do that. Not even with the way you're treating me right now." His mom and dad came back from the cafeteria with a bag of things. When Mom gave the girls an apple apiece, he declined to have one. Mom asked him what was going on. "This one, Cybill, hasn't spoken to me since she got here. But I think Jilly here is making up for it by being nasty and accusatory at me. Like I'd hurt any of them. Oh, and she's accused me of planning to dump her someplace when I take their older sister as my slave."

"What a thing to say to my son." Mom sat down by Jilly and asked Cybill to come closer. Of course, she just sat there. "When I tell you to come to me, you'll do it. I'm going to be your grandma, and I do expect you to respect me as an elder. You don't have to like me, but I'd like you to. Otherwise, you're going to find yourself at the wrong end of my heart. Now, come here so I can tell you what is going on with your sister. And what I would like to see happen to the two of you."

Cybill came to sit next to his mom, and Dad sat with him across from them. Mom told them that Lucy had a bad sprain on her wrist, and they were going to set it with a cast. Cybill told Mom they didn't have the money for that.

Ian spoke up. "I spoke to the bursar's office before you got here. All the bills are going to be sent to me. There won't be many of them, since as a family we've donated a great deal of money to this hospital in order to have the best of the best here. Lucy is in good hands." Jilly asked him where he lived. "About a twenty-minute drive from here. Not too far. I'm thinking they more than likely will keep her overnight simply because she'll need more in the way of pain medication than they can send her home with. I'd very much like it if you two were checked out. I know you said you didn't want to be but think of this. If you have a cold or some other sort of illness, you might make your sister weaker. They'll keep her longer if that happens. I'm not blackmailing you into anything, but I'm not too keen on either of you being sick either."

Cybill stood up, and so did Ian. She was so stiff it worried him. Was she hurt? Did something happen to the three of them to make them like this, other than being abandoned like they were? Ian wondered how soon his sisters would be able to track down the uncle.

"I'd like to make sure we don't have anything that would make Lucy sicker. She's all we have." Ian didn't point out that they had him too. He was working hard at making them believe in him before he tried to convince them he was going to be there for them. "But I'm not going to allow you in the room with me."

"Of course, I won't go into the room with you. Christ, kid, I'm not sure where your mind is all the time, but if you give me half a chance, you're going to see that I'm nothing like whoever shit in your oatmeal." Mom told him to behave. "Tell her that. I've done nothing to either of them, but try my best to show them I'm not the bad guy in this."

"Be that as it may, son. They're terrified and untrusting. We have to work on one thing at a time here."

He nodded and went to the desk. Jilly came with him. Instead of asking her what she wanted, he asked the nurse if there was someone who could look the girls over to make sure nothing was hurting them.

Ian turned to Jilly. "I'd very much like for my mom to go back with the two of you. She can keep in contact with me through our link. Just in case the nurses or doctors ask you for something that you might not understand." Jilly looked at her sister, then nodded to him. "Thank you for that. I know how hard it is for you to trust us. But I swear to you, we only have your best interests at heart."

"I don't trust you." Ian told her that was fine. Hopefully, she would someday. "What are your plans for us? Sending us away won't get you in good with my sister."

"I don't have any plans for you and your sister, other than wanting you safe and healthy. I want to take care that your uncle, wherever he is, knows he's messed up badly by treating you the way he has. Also, and this is true for my entire family, I'd very much like for you not to jump to the wrong conclusions about everything we say to you." Jilly's cheeks brightened up a little, and she turned away from him.

"Is there anything wrong with you, Jilly? I mean, are you hurt in any way that the doctors are going to find? I'd really like to know."

She turned to him then. While she looked at him with such intensity, he let her. Whatever she was thinking, he was sure it wouldn't bode well for him to try and read her mind. He was determined to allow her to make this call on her own.

"Three weeks ago, we were sleeping in a van. It wasn't nearly as bad as the one we've been in lately, but that's not saying much. It was all we could find at the time." He nodded. "There were no bathrooms, of course, so we had to go outside and do our business. Someone hit me from behind. I didn't lose consciousness, but I did get hit hard enough to draw blood. I still have trouble seeing things clearly, and I seem to have a headache all the time."

"Did you tell your sisters?" She shook her head gently. "All right. I'm going to go back with you to tell them what you've just told me. Also, I'd like to get my sisters-in-law involved. One of them is freaky scary magically powerful. However, she'd never harm either of you. She can find someone just by touching something. I don't know if she can with a head wound or not, but it's worth a try. Okay?"

"Why are you really doing this? Lucy won't care how much you say you're going to keep us safe. The first time something happens, you'll not find us." He told her he would now. "Because of you being a bear? I don't believe you."

"Believe me or not, Jilly, I'm a man of my word. If I tell you something I'll do or have done for you, I'll do it. I can find you because I have your scent. It won't be as easy as it would be if I had a taste of your blood, but you don't trust me enough for that. Not yet." She said she doubted she ever would. "I'm sorry for that. I truly am."

The nurse came to get the two girls, and he went back with them to wait for the doctor to come in the little room they were in. He'd asked the doctor, a woman he'd known for a while, Hallie Jamison, if the girls could be in the same area, as they're still frightened of him. He knew her from helping set up some of the computers they now had. Hallie laughed.

"You go on with you, Ian. I've got them here. They'll not be bothered." Ian told her what had happened to Jilly and how he was worried about her. "Head wound, huh? Well, you let me have a looksee at it, honey, and I'll see what I can get going for you right away."

Hallie had a gentle touch, but he could tell it was still painful for Jilly. Taking her hand into his, Ian held it tightly as Jilly tried her best not to cry. Cybill held her other hand. When Hallie stepped back, she looked at him. He could tell the news wasn't going to be good.

"She's got herself a piece of something under the skin. I don't know what it is right now. Not unless she can tell me what it was that hit her." Jilly told them she didn't know. There hadn't been anyone around. "I'm thinking you did lose consciousness for a little bit, honey. Not long, but long enough for whoever hit you to hit you a second time there. I found two places where the skin was broken. Whoever it was, they left you to die."

"But she'll be all right, won't she? Whatever it takes for her to be better, you do it, Hallie. I don't want anything to hurt them again." Jilly looked at him when he spoke to the doctor. "Just tell me what you're going to need to do to remove whatever is in her head."

"Nothing, Ian. You did good just getting this sort of information from her. She'll be right as rain." Hallie looked at Jilly. "I'm going to have them X-ray your head, honey. After we have a look at the films that come back, we'll be in a better position to figure out where we'll go from here. In the meantime, I'm going to give you a little something to make you relax a little. Being tense is not helping your head, I'm betting."

As soon as she left to get whatever was going to be needed for Jilly, Ian asked Cybill the same thing he'd asked Jilly. She told him she was always being babied by the other two, and she was never alone. Ian thought while she resented it a little, Cybill was glad not to be hurting like her sister.

"I'm going to check on Lucy while you're getting X-rays, all right?" Cybill said she didn't want to leave her sister. "I don't think they'll allow you in the room when they do that. However, they're going to bring her back to this area, and you and I will be here waiting for her. My mom will be, as well."

"I don't want either of them hurting." Ian told her he didn't either. "What will happen to me if they have to stay here? I can't go home with you. Not without my sisters."

"I know that. I never thought to make you leave them. I'll make a few calls, and we'll make sure, if we can, that all three of you are in the same room. If not, then you can move back and forth between their rooms to make sure they're all right. Would that be all right?" Cybill nodded, her big blue eyes dark with fear. "Good. Now, I'm going to reach out to my family with my link to them. You won't know I'm talking to them, but I promise you I'll tell you everything I find out, even about your uncle. I won't keep things from you guys. Ever, if I can help it."

Ian reached out to Demi first, telling her what he knew about the girls. She told him she was looking into the uncle for them and was looking for someone that might have a copy of the original will.

I don't for a minute think anyone would have left their children in his care if what they're saying is true. We have to assume this could be just a case of the girls not wanting to be around him. I'm not going to jump to conclusions. He told her that was a good idea. *Meadow is here with me. She's doing her thing too to find out what she can about the accident that killed their parents. Also, you should be aware that Melody is clothing shopping. They're going to need more than what they currently have even if they take off again. I don't think they will, but with kids, you never know.*

Thank you for that. I would like for Meadow to figure out what happened to Jilly that gave her the wound she has. Demi said she'd have her look. *Another thing—is there any way you can have someone go to my house and fill up the cabinets and fridge? I wasn't expecting anyone, and now I have three mouths to feed. I'm thrilled to death about it, but I also don't want them to think I'm planning to starve them.*

Closing the connection when Demi said she'd take care of it, he watched as a young aide took the bed out of the room to take Jilly to X-ray. Mom and Dad both joined them in the room while they waited.

"Do you think she'll die?" Mom told Cybill she didn't think either of her sisters would die. "I don't want them to. They're all I have left as my family."

"You have all of us now, Cybill. I want you to know that right off." Dad took the child's hand into his much larger one. "Yes, ma'am, you've got all of us now, and we're not going to let anyone hurt you again. Nor will you ever have to sleep in some old van. Unless it's a camping trip — then that'll be fine. You ever camp?"

Dad and Cybill spoke quietly while Mom peppered Ian with questions. Nothing he could answer for her, but it didn't stop her from asking. Mom went with Cybill to get her checkup while he and his dad waited. They didn't speak much. Ian was worried for his new family, and Dad seemed to be content with watching whatever was on the television while they waited.

When Lucy was finished with her arm being set, he went to see her in the room right next door. Telling her everything that was going on, he could see she was in a great deal of pain. When the nurse came in to give her something more for it, Ian stayed with her. She was asleep in a matter of minutes.

~*~

"I've removed the bullet without any trouble, but I still want to keep her for a couple more days just to make sure there is nothing more with the wounds. It's a small wonder she was having trouble seeing and a massive headache." Lucy didn't have any idea who would have shot her sister. Fearful of whoever it was coming for her again had her reaching out and grabbing the closest thing to her. It just happened to be Ian's warm hand. The doctor continued. "She's quite the trooper, I have to say. Not only was she fantastic at following instructions on what I needed her to do while I removed the bullet, she asked me questions about the procedure while it was happening to her."

"You mean she was awake?" Her voice squeaked, but she didn't care. They'd made her suffer through this without putting her out? "Isn't that sort of cruel?"

"Oh, no, Ms. Jackson. She didn't feel anything until I was ready for her to. When working with the brain or the skull, we want patients to be able to tell us if there is a change in their vision or speech. This way, if something were to have changed for her, Jilly was still in the operating room, and we could fix it immediately. She didn't have any trouble at all. Jilly even told me while we were working that she could see a little better."

"I don't understand." Ian turned to her, asking her what it was she needed clarification on. "Who would have shot her? Why? We weren't hurting anyone where we were. Why didn't she tell me she'd been hurt? I'm supposed to be taking care of them."

When the doctor left them, Ian sat in the chair next to her bed. Lucy wasn't sure what he was doing there, but it did occur to her that having him close was making her feel safer than she had at any time in the last year.

"I'm having my sister-in-law look into the shooting. The police have allowed her to touch the bullet. I did tell you she has some kind of thing going on with her mind, didn't I?" Lucy said he'd not explained that either. "All right. Do you remember the Spring murders? When the entire family was murdered except for one daughter?"

"Yes. They thought for a long time that it was her that killed them all. Even the dog, I believe." Ian told her that was it. "Are you telling me Meadow is that woman?"

"I am. When she was cut up like she was, her body sort of woke up some kind of mental ability. She can do all sorts of things we're still learning about. She was hoping that with her touching the bullet, she could backtrace the reason for it being shot at your sister and who might have done it." Lucy's head was spinning, and Ian seemed to understand she was overwhelmed. "When she has information, she said she'd tell me or come by, and I'll tell you without holding anything back. I'm going to be as honest and as straight up with you as I can. All right?"

"Yes. Do you know why she told you she'd been shot and not me?" He nodded. "I don't know why, but I have a feeling I'm not going to like the answer, am I?"

"I don't know if you will or not. But I do understand her motive for it. She thought you had enough on your plate, she told my dad, and she thought having a headache all the time was minor compared to what was going on in your lives. She would have told you, Jilly said, when you were safe, but it never seemed to be a good time to speak about it. Also, she had no idea she'd been shot. Jilly thought she'd been hit in the head with something."

"What about my other sister? What has Cybill been holding back from me?" Lucy hated the way she sounded as soon as she spoke. Ian had been nothing but nice to her, and here she was snipping and snapping at him. "I'm sorry. I'm trying to deal with this. I don't know you or what you are going to want from me. What you're going to do with my sisters, either. It's too much, but I know I have to deal with it. Deal with you."

"Dealing with me is going to be easy. I don't want anything from you or your sisters that you're not willing to give. I'm going to care for the three of you. As for what I'm going to do with them? I don't have any plans to do anything with them. I've provided them with rooms at our house. They have clothing now that my sisters-in-law got for them. As soon as you're up and around, we'll take them to get more. It's only fall now, so we'll have to look for winter things too, I guess. I don't know a great deal about teenage girls, to be honest with you. But I'm so very proud of you for keeping them safe and together."

"The doctor said we are all undernourished. I thought he was going to take them from me when he said that. But all he said was that with the cook you have at your house now, we'll be fattened up soon enough. I don't even know what that means." Ian laughed, and she felt a smile pull at her mouth. "You have money, don't you?"

"I do. I also have a home, a great job, and insurance that you and the girls have been added to as of this afternoon. I don't know a great deal about any of you, but I'm assuming you drive." She nodded and told him she had a license, but it had been taken from her at her uncle's. "They've found him, by the way. Demi isn't going to contact him until she figures out a few things about him. I'm not sure what those are, but she said she'd have you some information soon."

"They're very resourceful, aren't they?" Ian laughed and told her that was an understatement. "What will they do with my uncle now that they know where he is? I mean, it's not like my sisters and I have any recourse. I've been so worried he was going to come after us and ditch me in order to keep them around. I suppose he could. I'm an adult, and they're not."

"I did mention that to the others. Mr. Shoe is an attorney for the family right now. Mostly Demi, but he's looking into what can and can't be done. You told me you didn't know where the will was. If you can tell me where your parents died, then we can go there and find their death certificates and work backward from there." She told him everything she knew, which, after saying it aloud, she thought was a pitiful amount of information. "Once they know where to look, finding it will be easy. I mean, they would have filed it in order for it to be legal and binding."

"I have some questions for you. I know you're telling me I'm your mate, but how do I know you're not trying to scam me into your home and bed? For all I know, you could be a murderer or a rapist. I don't want to go from the pot to the fire without knowing what I'm getting into." He told her that was fair, then to ask him whatever she wanted. "I don't know what to ask you. I don't know you at all."

"Nor do I know you, Lucy. But I'm a college graduate of the local college. I have a computer science degree that is helping me while I learn what Demi and Meadow have me do. I can, and do most of the time, build computers for the elite.

All the family is now the owner of a great many properties all over the world, and I keep the computers working so Demi's cameraman, my brother, can install cameras and keep them as well as anything else in the homes up and running." She asked him about his house. "Ah, there is a funny story to that. Demi and Meadow purchased the houses for all of us a while back. All I've done to it since moving in was throw a mattress on the floor and look for things to fill it a little at a time. It has nine bedrooms. Also, I've managed to find a couple of ponies I'm working with so they're not afraid of me. I'm not a rancher by any stretch of the imagination, but I'm having fun just hanging around the place when I'm not working."

"Nine bedrooms is a huge house." He told her about the kitchen and how it was supposed to be a cook's dream. "You don't cook."

"No. I mean, I know how, but I don't unless I'm too hungry to wait until I can hang out at my mom's house for a meal." He grinned at her. "When I first figured out the three of you would need a place to stay, I had my mom and sisters go and fill the place up with food. While I don't have any idea what they purchased, I'm sure it's going to be a good mixture of good for you things as well as fun food. My mom is a wonderful cook. I'm to understand that you love to bake."

"I do. I'm good at it too. Not tooting my own horn, but I used to have people come from everywhere to have some of the breads and cakes I make." Ian had the most generous smile. When he smiled, it was like he was telling her he was as happy as he could be. "I don't know what I'm supposed to do with you."

"With me? I don't know either. As I said, I'm not going to rush you. I'll take whatever you wish to give me. However, I plan to pamper you so much, you'll wish to bash my head in."

This time she laughed. Laying her head back on the pillow, she watched as he explained to her what sort of pampering he was planning to do.

When the door to her room opened, she was so happy to see Cybill that she had her climb into the bed with her, simply so she could make sure she was all right. Ian didn't make fun of her, nor did he scold her sister for climbing over her and causing her pain. Lucy thought he would have for some reason.

"I'm going to go and check on Jilly if you two will be all right." Lucy thanked him. "You can have anything you want to eat. Would you like me to pick you two up something and bring it to you? The sky's the limit."

"I would love a hamburger. With everything." Ian told Cybill he could get her that, then asked her about fries. "No, I don't care for potatoes. But if they have onion rings, I'd really enjoy that. Are you sure you don't mind getting it for me?"

"I'm positive. I'm hoping we can be a family. But I'll settle for good terms for now." Lucy told him she'd like the same, but she liked fries. None of them liked soda, so he was going to bring them back bottled waters. "I'll be back. If there is anything I find out about Jilly, I'll let you know that too."

When he was gone, Cybill told her she liked the McCray family. "You've been getting to know them, I guess." Cybill said mostly she'd been with Grandpa McCray, but Grandma was nice too. "You're already calling them your grandparents? Cybill, do you think that's a good idea? We shouldn't get too attached to them right now. Don't you think?"

"I don't think that at all. We're warm and getting taken care of, Lucy. I've been checked out and given a vitamin D shot so I could be better. You've had your arm looked at and fixed. Jilly is getting taken care of, and tonight, when I go to bed, I'll have a roof over my head, a bed to sleep in, and a bathroom all my own." She asked her where she was staying. "I've been taken by the grandparents to Ian's house. You're going to love it, Lucy. It's so beautiful, and I can't wait to live there for the rest of my life."

Lucy was worried that something was going to happen to take all these plans away from them. A roof over their head was a good thing, but at what cost? When she thought of all the things that Ian or the rest of them could demand of them, Lucy had a feeling they'd not want anything in return. They were, she hoped, just what they looked like—a good family with no ulterior motive of any kind.

Chapter 2

Demi looked over all the paperwork she'd been gathering and couldn't understand how anyone would have thought Josh Jackson should have not just been given custody of the three children of Lucille and Donald Jackson, but also access to their money.

"Can I help you?" She smiled at Lucian. "I've been watching you for the last ten minutes, and I can't believe I've never noticed how you make faces when you're upset with something you're reading."

"This is so fucked up I can't believe that no one has done something about it. I've figured out several things about their uncle. First and foremost, I would have killed him before I'd allow him to talk to one of my children." Lucian asked her what she'd found out. "He's been in prison twice now. Once for writing bad checks—I'm talking thousands upon thousands of dollars' worth. The second time was for using stolen credit cards. Do you see the trend here?"

"So how did he manage to get this nice gig?" She told him she was working on that. "Is there any money left for the girls? I'd hate to think he's left them without anything."

"No. He's not been able to get to the bulk of it, but not for lack of trying. The large allotment check he gets every month is a good deal of money. He's banking it, or he was. I think he figured that someday someone would figure out he's been lying to people, and he was making himself a nice nest egg. He's also trying to sell the family home, which, I might add, isn't a small piece of property. Six thousand acres, as well as a mansion of a home. But I don't think the attorneys for the estate have any idea he's unloaded the kids on the side of the road." Lucian asked her what she was doing about it. "Lots of things at the moment. I'm having the money moved to an account that I set up in the girls' names. I also put Ian on it in the event someone tries to say Ian was in it for the cash. I called him to come here just before you came in. I'm surprised he's not here yet."

"He's here. That was what I came in here to tell you. He has Cybill and Lucy with him. Jilly is doing better, I've been told, and should be home in the next couple of days." She nodded and stood up. "You have a plan, don't you? Is it going to make this Josh person come out of the woodwork after them?"

"More than likely, yes. There are things that Ian and Lucy need to do to make things legal too. Like getting married, then adopting her sisters." Lucian followed her into the den where they were. Lucy already looked better than she had the other night. And Cybill looked like she was ready to bounce off the walls, she was so energetic. "I have some news for you three that I'm not sure how you're going to take. But in order for the three of you to stay together in this, I think, along with my attorney, that it's better to be prepared for the worst than to let it come then try dealing with it. I would like to suggest that you and Ian get married as soon as it could possibly be arranged. Then you can—"

"Wait. Just wait. How is me getting married to a man I hardly know going to keep my sisters with me? I'm assuming that's what you mean." Demi said it was. "I'm not marrying a stranger for any reason."

"Okay. But here is the situation. Even if you were no longer under the care of your uncle, someone is going to have to raise Cybill and Jilly until they're adults. I'm not saying you're a bad person, but a court could say you weren't a good role model for them because you were the oldest and had them living on the streets without medical attention or proper meals. I know you did the best you could, but the courts will try anything to get things to go in the direction of the kids not being with you. They'll also receive part of the estate as compensation for taking care of them. That will be what they want. And there is no way to make sure that once they're in the system, they'll be able to stay together." Lucy asked her if she adopted them by herself if that would work. "Again, it's going to be looked at that you were living on the streets. If you're not married, where will you live? How will you care for them without any means to keep them safe? How will you work with no address? These are things they're going to take into consideration when you ask to adopt them. I'm not saying this is going to happen, Lucy, but I'd count on it transpiring. Good people rarely get a break when dealing with some of the people in these sorts of organizations."

Lucy looked at Ian. "I don't want to marry you." Ian only nodded. He was a good man, but she could see he was hurting about this as well. "How will you feel if I say yes, and you know I don't want to do this?"

"How would you feel if you were forced into a corner? I'm not saying marrying you will be any kind of hardship for me. I've already fallen in love with your sisters, and I very much would love to get to know you. But for the sake of your family, I can't think of a better way for them to be with you and I." He looked at Demi then. "Demi, what will happen to their uncle when it comes out that he's been stealing from the estate? Because from what you told me earlier, he's not been doing anything legal."

"I've located the will. It's pretty standard when it mentions you and your sisters' care. It says if your parents were to die before any of you are old enough to take care of the others, then you would be put in the temporary care of the staff of the household. I didn't know how much of a staff you had, but it looks like they've made sure the people in the house were well equipped to handle any situation." Lucy asked her how her uncle was involved. "From what I've seen, he wasn't even mentioned in the will. I do have someone looking for an amendment to the original will. So far, there isn't one. Also, the house is yours until such time that your sisters are old enough to decide how they wish to divide it."

"So, I have a place to live with them if I want to adopt them." Demi told her she did. That wasn't going to be the issue. It was the state wanting their share. "Why can't I just tell them no? I mean, I know we've been homeless for some time now, but that's not my fault."

"Did you go to the police? Did you contact your father's attorney? They're going to ask you these questions too. And if you didn't, why not?" Lucy looked so defeated that it hurt Demi a little that she couldn't make it work out for her. "I'm so sorry, Lucy. If I could figure out a way for this to work in a different way, I'd tell you."

"I don't want to have to marry for this. It's like I'm being forced into something not of my choosing." Ian told her she was right. "You're not going to be hurt by this. Why are you even commenting?"

He didn't say anything when he looked at her. Demi could see the pain on his face. So when he stood up and left the room, she didn't say anything to him. Neither did she when she stood up. Cybill apparently had no such trouble talking to her sister.

"What the hell is wrong with you? You have a nice man helping you out with keeping us all together, and you toss him away like he is nothing at all. Don't you see how this is nothing he wants, either?" Lucy told her sister it was none of her concern. "Isn't it? Are you telling me that since you're the oldest, you hold all the cards? That you aren't going to take into consideration how we feel about what happens to you and to us?"

Cybill stood up and left them there. The front door

slamming had Lucy flinching at the sound. When she started to cry, Demi didn't say anything to her, but let her muddle through this on her own. When Lucy looked up at her, Demi just waited for whatever came out of her mouth next.

"I'll do it. If this is my only option, I guess I'll have to." Demi didn't want to tell her she'd have to convince Ian now. She also didn't want to tell her the family was going to be none too happy with her after it got out that she'd pissed off Ian so much he'd left them sitting there. "Aren't you going to gloat? Tell me I'm stupid for trying to keep my family together and safe by living on the streets? Go ahead. You might as well beat me up with my actions too."

"Nah, you're doing a fine job all on your own." Demi stood up when the baby started to roll around, making her slightly uncomfortable to sit for very long. "I will tell you this. You hurt any of the rest of the family, as you just did the nicest man I know, then I'll make sure your little family suffers in ways your uncle hasn't even begun to think about."

Demi went to her office and closed the door. She was emotional. The baby also made her sleep poorly, and that wasn't helping. Standing at the door, she cried as quietly as she could while her heart hurt her in ways she'd not ever felt before. Demi was hurting for Ian more than anyone else right now.

I have a question for — What's happened? She told Alden she was all right, just emotional. *You're not all right, my dear. I can feel your pain all the way to my toes. Tell me who to slay, and I'll do it.*

She told him everything. Even how Lucy had made her

feel about helping her. Alden was kindhearted when he told her she was emotional too. That things were kind of messy on Lucy and the girls' end as well. While she understood that, she told Alden it didn't mean she had to be nasty about them helping her.

Tell me something. Would you have been happy if someone told you that you most definitely had to marry Lucian if you ever wanted to see that baby of yours? That as soon as it was born, it would be taken from you for no other reason than someone thought you're a bad person? She pointed out to him that she'd not said it. *Yes, I'm sure you didn't. But when you're hurting, pushed into something you don't want or think you need, and someone is taking your money, don't you think that is what it would feel like?*

She thought about it and decided perhaps he was correct. That it wasn't just emotions that were making Lucy upset and saying things she wouldn't normally say, but also that she'd not had a single bit of control over any of the things going on around her. Not to mention her sister being shot and her being in pain as well. It was a great deal to be tossing at anyone, especially when it was all things Lucy literally had no control over. She asked Alden when he'd gotten so smart.

I'd say I was like this all the time, but there are people out there that would dispute that. They'd have something smart to say about me. I don't give a good piece of fudge about it. I want you to know I'm not a bragger about it either. She said she loved him for that. *And I love you too, my darling. You need to cry on my shoulder again, and I'll be right here for you.*

When he told her he had to go, she almost reminded him he'd wanted to ask her something. But she knew she was going to have to clear the air between her and Lucy. They were going to be related, and Demi didn't want any bad blood between the two of them. Also, she didn't want the younger girls to dislike her. They might make the perfect sitters someday.

Lucy was asleep, tears still staining her cheeks when she saw her. Getting one of the blankets that were forever in a large basket in the corner, she covered her up with it. Lucy came up fighting. Demi was glad she'd not been too close when Lucy swung out to hit whoever startled her awake.

"I'm sorry." Demi told her it was fine, then asked her if she could talk to her. "I've fucked up. I have been bounced around, taking care of my sisters for so long by myself, I've forgotten how to be polite. I'm so very sorry."

"I'm an emotional mess myself. As much as I hate to admit this to anyone, I'm barely hanging on most days. Having a baby can sure make you say and do things you'd not normally do." Lucy told her she was just a bitch, and didn't have anyone to blame it on like a baby. "Oh, I'd say you have plenty to blame on your uncle. If you're ready to listen to me, I can tell you what I've done to ensure that you and your sisters aren't broke when you get things moving back to normal."

"Do you think that is ever going to happen? Besides, what is normal anyway?" They both laughed. "I'm truly sorry, Demi. I know you're all working and doing things to keep us from being completely homeless. I know, too, that I have to talk to Ian. I hurt him with my temper, and that wasn't my intention."

"He's a good man. Not that I'm saying this to change your mind, but you couldn't do better with him in your corner.

Ian isn't like most men you'll meet. None of the McCrays are. They're good people." Lucy told her she was getting that impression too. "Good. Let me fill you in on what I've been able to get going for the three of you. I hate to bring this up again, but you're going to be much better off marrying Ian as soon as possible. Even as bad as your uncle is, it could come to the point where he calls you unfit, and if that happens, you're pretty much screwed if anyone finds out how you've been living lately."

"Won't they already know that?" Demi told her her plan. "So you'd lie for us. Tell everyone we've been living here with the family to get our feet back under us since we were abandoned so carelessly. Would that work?"

"Oh yes. Especially if we can back it up with a marriage." Lucy asked her to explain things about Josh so she could absorb the rest of what she was saying. "Great. I've stolen back all the money your uncle has stolen from you."

~*~

Ian was browning a large roast when he heard someone behind him. Turning slowly, careful not to shift, he looked at Cybill as she stood there in the doorway. Not saying anything to her, he turned back to his job. She'd either stay or not. He didn't care much anymore.

"Can I help you?" He told her there were potatoes and carrots that needed to be peeled. "I'm not entirely sure how to do that, but I'm willing to learn. I like your house, by the way."

"Thanks. It's sort of bare right now, but then I wasn't expecting anyone to come live with me." He got her a peeler and some potatoes and carrots out of the bin. "My mom grew the carrots, and I got the potatoes from a roadside market yesterday. I think if you peel a lot, we can have leftovers if you want to hang around."

"I do. I've been thinking about a lot of things that are going on. I think because I'm the youngest, they think I'm deaf or something. I heard my sisters talking, and it was harder living out on the streets than I think people realize." He told her he was sorry for that. "Yeah, me too. Uncle Josh, he really screwed us over. But then, I never liked him, even when he stayed at my parents' home for a little while. Dad had to kick him out when he caught him bringing women to the house."

"That was ballsy of him. I mean, your uncle." Ian turned to look at Cybill after putting the roast in the oven to cook. "I know nothing about girls. I don't know how to be a parent to you if that's what you need. Nor do I have any idea how I'm supposed to talk to you. I'm sure you've been around cussing before, but is it right to do that in front of a fifteen-year-old?"

"Probably not. But then, my mom could curse like it was her job when she was upset." They both laughed. "I'm sorry for how my sister treated you. That wasn't at all nice of her. But she has been putting up with a lot of stuff trying to keep us from being raped nightly and having at least a little food once a day. She didn't do too bad of a job."

"No, she didn't. The fact that you're still alive goes to show how much she's done for you guys. She should be very proud of herself for that." Cybill told him that wasn't something Lucy was good at. "What? You mean being proud of herself?"

"Not Lucy. She will almost always find fault with what she's done. Lucy is harder on herself than anyone around. Also, you should know she's terrible at jokes. She is too logical, my dad used to tell her. I think she's a stick in the mud. Are you going to have this for dinner tonight?" He told her they both could if she wanted to join him, but she had to tell her sister where she was. "I can do that. She's been really stressed out, you know?"

"I can only imagine."

Cybill didn't say anything more after nodding. Ian picked up a carrot and started to trim it down to bite sizes as he waited on her to come to terms with whatever she was thinking.

"When my parents were killed, Lucy came home. She'd been living on her own for a while by then. She's super smart and is the best baker I've ever known. I know that's not saying much as I'm only a kid, but to me, it was amazing to see her putting ingredients together and getting a beautiful loaf of bread or a cake." She didn't look up at him as she got up to get something to drink. "They were taking a second honeymoon—my parents, I mean. They were having a good time, they told us when they called us nightly. Jilly and I were at home with the staff then. The calls stopped suddenly. After three days of not hearing from them, Jilly called Lucy to tell her what was going on. She dropped everything and came to us."

"What happened to them?" Cybill poured them both a glass of tea, then sat across from him. Ian got the tin of cookies his mom had given him yesterday and opened them between them. "You said they were killed. Were they murdered?"

"Not really. Not in an evil sort of way. We were told they were taking a hike through one of the many wooded areas where they were, and something attacked them both. It took us a while to figure out that wasn't true either. They'd been caught in a rainstorm that had the mountain coming down on top of them." Ian told her he was sorry. "Yeah. The reason it took them so long to call us, because the police did eventually, was that they were still digging the little town out that Mom and Dad were staying in. We couldn't even bring them home for burial. Something about they were afraid of any kind of disease they could bring back to the States. They'd been buried for about ten days when they were found."

"I'm so sorry." Cybill told him they had been doing what they liked doing, being together and having a nice walk in the woods. "I enjoy that, as well. I think as my bear, I enjoy it much more. Are you afraid of me? With me being a bear?"

"No. I don't believe you'd hurt me. Not on purpose anyway. I don't know that for sure, but you don't strike me as a person that would just be mean to someone because of what you are." He laughed when she smiled at him. "I would like to tell you something about my sister. Lucy is a strong person. She's usually very easy to get along with and to talk to. But with all this, all the things that have been happening, she's stressed out to the point where I worry about her having a heart attack or something."

"I don't want to hurt her either." Cybill told him she didn't think he would, but that Lucy had hurt him. "She did. But once I got away and came here, I got to thinking about what you just said. She's getting a lot of crap thrown at her that she doesn't have a great deal of say over. Like your uncle."

"Josh never was a nice person. One year for Christmas he got my sister and I a doll each. Three days after he left for greener pastures, as he told us, the police came by and told us it was stolen goods, and we had to give them up. They also wanted to know if we had any idea where Josh was." Ian told her he sounded like a peach. "Yeah, with mostly pit. After that, whenever he came bearing gifts again, we'd just put them aside and waited for someone to want them back. Finally, Dad told him not to come back with anything. Also, he'd like it if he didn't come around at all. Once they were dead, however, Josh came to the house and told us that, according to the will, he'd been deemed our guardian. That we were to do what he told us and not bitch about it. He was, he told us, in charge of our lives from then on. Uncle Josh then said he was going to take over all the companies my parents had. That didn't happen, by the way. I don't know what happened, but he never did a thing with any of the companies."

"What happened after he moved into the house?" Cybill told him how they'd been taken to the mall in the family limo. "What did he say to you when he was taking you there? I mean, was it his intention of leaving you there from the start?"

"Yes. Oh yeah, that's what he was planning. When we got there, he said for us to go on in and he'd join us in a bit. Lucy was sure he wasn't going to do any such thing and argued with him about how we were her responsibility. He slugged her in the face, knocking her out, then shoved her out of the car. It was a while before she came around, but by then, the mall had closed up, and we had nothing."

Ian was going to kill the fucker when he saw him. Cybill smiled at him as she continued the story. Mostly it was how they'd wandered around for a few days, eating what they could find. His heart broke for the three of them. Ian couldn't imagine how they were able to survive after all they'd been through.

Between the two of them, they got dinner ready to be finished up. It was too soon to put the veggies in, so he turned the oven down low and put everything they'd readied in the fridge. He asked her then if she wanted to find Lucy. He wanted to tell her how sorry he was.

"She's going to be all right, isn't she, Ian? I know she can be a pain in the butt, but really, she's so stressed out all the time." Ian told her he was only going to offer her the house. "You won't live here with us? I have to tell you, I really love this place. I already picked out my room when Grandma Cindy brought us by earlier."

"Good for you. One less thing I need to worry about. I'm going to get you some furniture, but we have to make sure Lucy is all right with you and your sister staying here. In answer to your question, no, I won't live here with you guys until your sister is comfortable with me being around. I don't want to add to her stress any more than I want her to be hurt." Cybill told him she didn't either. "All right. Let's get going. On the way back to my brother's house, you can tell me more about this soon to be dead uncle of yours."

Cybill laughed. "You're what my grandma called a corker, aren't you? I like you, Ian. Very much." He told her he liked her as well. "Now all we have to do is convince my sister that she's going to be much better off with you hanging around than not. I don't think you're going to have an easy time of it, just so you know."

"Kid, I live for things not being easy."

They were both still laughing as they went out the front door. Lucian was just pulling into his front drive. Lucy got out on the other side as Lucian told him he was glad he was still here.

"What's going on? Did something happen to Jilly?"

Lucian told him to talk to Lucy and returned to his car and left them. Lucy stood where she'd gotten out of the car and didn't move. Cybill asked her if she was hungry.

"Ian and I made a roast for dinner. It's not done yet, but we've been talking. Are you going to be nasty to him again?" Lucy told her sister she wasn't. "Good. I'm going to go to my room now and figure out what sort of things I'd like to have in it. And so you know, Lucy, I'm still mad at you for talking to him the way you did." True to her word, Cybill left them there.

"Would you like to come in? I have a couch and some chairs in the living room. Not much else. I was planning to fill it as I went, but if you have any ideas as to how you want it to look, then—"

"I'm sorry about how I spoke to you." He nodded and told her he was sorry too. "For what? Being a nice guy? I guess I could also tell you I'm not used to having people be nice to me. I'm usually much nicer than I've been today."

"I don't doubt it. Would you like to come in?" He opened the door for her but made sure he didn't get too close to her.

Lucy was as jumpy as a cat on a roof right now. When they were in the living room, she sat down on the couch and, unsure where he was to sit, he sat across from her. "I was telling Cybill I'd like for you and your sisters to live here. I can stay with one of my brothers while you figure out what you want to do about this. I'll support you in any way you want."

"Will you marry me?" He didn't even blink at the question. "I've had a very long conversation with Demi, as well as her attorney, Mr. Shoe. They kindly told me to keep my mouth shut and listen to all they had to say before I jumped to any conclusions."

"I bet Mr. Shoe was nice, but I don't see Demi doing that. She has a tendency to tell people what she thinks. Whether you want to hear it or not." Lucy smiled and said she was a little rougher than Mr. Shoe. "What did they tell you that they hadn't when I was there? More about your uncle, I'm betting. By the way, I'm going to kill him when I see him. There is no reason whatsoever why he should treat you three the way he has."

"I might just help you. On the way here, I've been making and tossing out all sorts of plans that would keep me from having to make you suffer through marrying me. There really isn't any way it will work where I get to make sure my sisters are all right." He said he was sorry. "Please don't be. I know I hurt you with what I said, but you really are a nice guy. I'm just being a bitch."

"What you're being is someone that is overwhelmed about things right now." He came to a sudden decision. "If you're serious about marrying me, Lucy, I can still bunk with one of my brothers. No one but my family has to know what we've arranged. And I know they won't say anything to anyone. I want you to be happy, but mostly I want you to be with your sisters and be safe."

"You'd do that for me? Without any questions or stipulations on it?" He told her he'd never do that to her. "I must have hit the lottery with your family. Ian, if you'd do me the honor of marrying me and keeping me and my sisters safe, I'd be forever grateful to you."

"All right. I'll make the arrangements and have Demi pull some strings. I'm betting we can get married tomorrow. If you'd like, we can do it at the hospital so Jilly can be there as well." She said she'd like that. "Good. Welcome to the family, Lucy. I'm so very glad we found each other."

As it turned out, Demi pulled some major strings, and they could get married that afternoon. He drove them to the hospital where Jilly was and had his family meet them there. It might not be a traditional wedding or marriage, but he planned on making up for it as the years went by — to all three of his girls.

Chapter 3

Josh was on the phone when someone tried to call him. Usually, he'd not get a call for days at a time—he'd be the one making all the calls. Then today, he'd had four in a row. As he was waiting on hold with the first call, he scrambled through his paperwork to figure out where his last receipt was. Damn it all to fuck, he was lost without his secretary helping him find things.

Last night he'd found his house empty of servants. Not a single one of them were in their homes that his brother had had put in for them. Their furniture was still there, but no clothing, no food, and certainly no servants. Even his own kitchen seemed to be devoid of anything to eat that he wanted to take the time to fix for himself.

The person on the other end came back on the line. "Yes, I'm trying to figure out the balance of my account. I've had some strange calls today, and I want to make sure there has been some sort of mistake on your end." The woman, he'd already dismissed her name from his head, told him they didn't make mistakes. "Come on now. That can't possibly be true. I mean, I'm checking my balance online here, and it says there isn't anything in my accounts."

"If you're looking online for your account information, why is it you're bothering me for the same information?" He told her it was wrong. "Perhaps it's you that is wrong. Give me the information once again, and I'll run it from here. Why you'd want it verified twice is beyond me when you have it right there."

Biting his tongue so he'd not piss her off more, he gave her not only the account number but also the date of his last deposit. On top of that, he gave her his date of birth, as well as his social security number. Then he was put on hold.

That was one of the most annoying things he'd encountered about having money. When he was broke, of course, he never called people demanding things. But with all the money in the world — well, a great deal of it — he was forever calling this person or that to make sure they were doing what they were supposed to do so he'd have money.

Then today. Josh hadn't any idea why the staff had left. There wasn't a single note anywhere that he could find. And he'd looked too. His dishes in the sink told him they'd not even cleaned up after him when he'd had his dinner. A dinner, he just realized that wasn't up to par.

The woman came back on the line. "As you are aware, the account is emptied except for one cent. I could close it out for you if that is your wish." He said he didn't want it closed, and asked her where his money was. "I'm sure I don't know, sir. It says on the account that you ordered the money to be moved to a second account just yesterday. I cannot help you any longer. Do not call here if you already have the correct answers."

Then she hung up on him. He wanted to throw his phone across the room, but sadly it was one of those that were connected to the wall and had cords running everywhere. Why his brother had a landline was beyond him. Josh was having to look up every phone number he wanted in the giant Rolodex beside the heavy assed thing.

Sitting down at his desk again, he ran his fingers through his hair and looked around. There wasn't a thing out of place. None of his passwords or account numbers had been disturbed either. Yet all his money was gone, his safe had been standing wide open, and the money and jewelry he'd found all over the house were missing. Who would have done such a thing and thought he'd not press charges?

He couldn't, he knew that. Not only could he not press charges on the missing things, but he couldn't have the police involved at all. They'd want to know where the children were, where the will was that had put him in charge of them and their money. Just yesterday morning, he'd been told that someone from the welfare office was going to be at this house on Friday to talk to the girls, and to see if Lucy, the oldest, had any comments on how things were going with the care of her sisters.

"That bitch has done this. I know it." Getting up to look again for something that would tell him where his things were, he kicked the newspaper across the room. The name Jackson was in bold letters across one of the pages and had him bending over to pick the paper up.

Reading it over three times, he decided he didn't know who the hell it was. There wasn't any mention of this Lucille person having any sisters. The man she was marrying had a name he'd never heard before. Tossing the paper aside, he went to figure out if there was a calendar in the kitchen that told him the entire household was on vacation.

"They'd better be. If they've left me, that is going to be the wrong move on their part." He didn't have any idea what sort of restrictions he could put on them if they were gone on a planned vacation. But he'd been talking to himself for so long now he figured if it came out of his mouth, it had to be right. He was smiling when he entered the kitchen again.

The woman sitting there at the table was no one he knew. Josh hoped she was some sort of replacement for his staff and asked her if she was there to cook for him. Instead of answering him, she continued to sip her tea and munch on what looked to him like giant biscuits. He reached for one of them.

"Touch that, and I'll remove your hand from the elbow down. Sit your ass down and keep your fucking mouth shut." He didn't feel like he had a choice in the matter and sat down. Once there, he thought about getting up, and the person glared at him. "I've been looking over some of your handy work, Josh. You're not going to get away with this."

"Oh yeah? What might you think you've been looking over?" She looked at him oddly, and he realized how stupid he sounded. "Tell me what you think I should be worried about with you. You're not supposed to be here, and that's breaking and entering."

She laid a set of keys on the table. They looked like the ones his brother had in his pocket all the time when he'd been alive. "Where did you get those? Do you have any idea how long I've been searching for the keys to his car?"

"I don't know. Why don't you enlighten me?" He didn't care for her tone but asked her again about the keys. "I have a better question for you, Josh. Why don't you tell me where the girls are? Do you ever go and check on them? I'm to understand you've dropped them off at the mall twice now. Where are you supposed to pick them up this time? The county welfare office is supposed to be here soon, aren't they?"

"What is it you think you know? And what I've done with those girls is really none of anyone's business. My brother told me to keep an eye on them, and I'm doing that." The woman told him he wasn't. "I am too. They're having a good time hanging out at the mall. Just like you said."

"I never said they were at the mall, moron. I simply pointed out that is where you dropped them off. Both times you had to have the household inspected by the county. I don't think you're going to have an easy time finding them this time. They've been gone for nearly eight months now. Wouldn't you say?" He didn't have any idea when it was he'd dropped them off at the mall. He did know he'd not had to hit Lucy when they'd gotten there this time. "About that. Did you know you cracked her jaw? That as of right now, she's going to have to have a brace put on the bone you hit.

Not very uncle-like of you, if you ask me."

"I didn't ask you shit. Why are you here? To ask me questions you already know the answer to?" Now he got why the woman on the phone was pissy with him. This woman asking questions she had the answers for was annoying. But then that was what the banker was getting paid for. "I want you out of my house right now."

"It's not your house. I've found the will, and you weren't even mentioned in it. Much less told to take the money earmarked for their children. Did you check your balance today?" She smiled. "I guess you did. It was fun, really, taking it out of your accounts and putting it into one that the three girls of Mr. and Mrs. Jackson can use. I wanted to personally thank you for not spending any of it. However, you should be gathering up the very little you came with and get out before I have to rough you up. The house and its contents, they don't belong to you."

"I haven't the slightest idea where you're getting your information, but I have the will in my office." She said it was his brother's office. "No. It used to be, but now it's mine. As is the care of his children and their money. I think it's about time you left here. Before I call the police."

"You won't do that. Calling the police could cause you all sorts of trouble, now couldn't it? They'd ask you questions about where the children are or even why you are trying to sell off the place when it's not even in your name. You thought there would be something for you in this, and came here fully aware that you were to stay away from the family and not to bother the girls ever again." She was dead right about everything. Instead of letting on that he was afraid of what she knew, Josh stood up and went to the back door. "Good for you. Leaving now while there's still time before the family arrives."

"I'm not leaving here. You are." She just smiled at him. "I haven't any idea why you think I'm joking, but this is my house, and I demand that you get out, right fucking now. I don't have time for this shit."

"Of course, you don't. You have little girls to find. Money to chase down. Things like that can wear a man down, I'm told." She stood up, and Josh realized how incredibly tall the woman was. When her face turned deadly, the only way he could have described how she stared at him, Josh swallowed twice before she spoke. "If I have to return here to move your ass out of here before the girls are ready to claim this home as their own, you're going to be farting from your ears, because your ass will be so curled up inside of you."

Then she just disappeared. Josh staggered to the table and sat down, nearly missing the chair twice before he realized they were all pushed under the table as if no one had been sitting there. When he looked around, he noticed there wasn't a teacup out of place or a single crumb on the table. Josh told himself over and over that it had been a bad dream. A terribly bad dream.

Sitting there for several more minutes, he was able to convince himself it had been just a bad dream for him. He had dozed off, and that was why it had seemed so real. Getting up then, feeling a lot like his old self, he looked for keys to any of the several cars in the garage to drive and find the girls. He had to find them. Tomorrow was going to be a big day, and they had to be there, or he'd be in trouble.

When he finally located keys, they were to his old beat-up POS, a junker he'd stolen and driven here when he'd gotten word that his brother and his wife were dead. He hated to be seen in such a piece of shit. However, he needed to get going. He figured the car was worth less than his worst pair of shoes, which was zip. And that was the reason no one had asked him where it had come from.

Getting the thing started enough to be put into gear, Josh was moving down toward the mall an hour later. There was going to have to be a better plan than the one he'd been relying on. Dropping them off at the mall had been a nice place for him, but then he'd have to search for hours trying to locate them when he needed them. Josh decided he was going to have them stay at the mall. Girls liked the mall, didn't they? It shouldn't be any sort of hardship for them to hang out there until he needed them again.

"Stupid children. Don't they have any idea how much work they're causing me? It's doubtful they even care." He was sure the youngest wouldn't. She was mouthy, and he couldn't stand to be around her, questioning every move he made. "I'll gag her as soon as I find her."

He thought about the oldest one. Josh had an idea she was older than the other two by a few years but was not sure how old she was. Remembering her tall slim body, he thought her to be about seventeen. No older than that, however. If she was, he was sure his brother would have mentioned it in his will that whatever her name was, she could take care of the kids instead of the staff.

"Which is really stupid. They'd be sucking them dry more than I am." But they'd have a house to live in, he thought. Not to mention food and warm clothing. "Then they should have prepared better after their parents were killed. That's what I'm going to tell them when I see them. That they had plenty of time between their mom and dad dying and me getting here to be ready to be homeless."

He was laughing so hard at his own joke that he nearly missed pulling into the mall. Josh sat there, staring at the place he'd dropped the girls off for a full ten minutes. Construction was going on everywhere. It was no longer a mall. In fact, there was a sign out front that proclaimed it to be the site for the new high school.

"What the hell?" He pulled forward enough that he could see there were construction workers all over the beams. The walls to it were mostly up, and he noticed there were no windows on the lower few feet of the place. "Who the hell said they could tear down the mall?"

Not that he ever went there. He couldn't remember the last time he'd shopped at any of the stores that used to be in the place. Trying to remember if he'd seen anything in the newspaper about all this shit, he was startled into screaming a little when someone knocked on his window.

"I have a truck coming in behind you." He didn't understand what the person wanted him to do, so he leaned over to roll down the window. "I need for you to move. You're holding up the trucks behind you, buddy. Just park someplace else."

He moved to what used to be the parking lot of the mall. The trucks, monster things, were lined up behind him three deep. Watching them go to the site, he marveled at how the people on the ground unloaded each of the beds of the trucks with heavy equipment he'd always wanted to learn how to drive.

He supposed all young boys wanted to be able to drive big equipment. Josh had been just like that, wanting to be a trucker or some other glamorous job that involved driving something huge like that. But he'd been a bum. At least until his brother died and he took over his estate.

~*~

Lucy wandered around the house, not really seeing much. Her mind was on what had happened tonight. She was a married woman with two sisters she was caring for, as well as an absent husband. Though the absent husband part was her own doing. She had asked him for time and he, sweetly, gave it to her.

"Whatcha doing?" Lucy looked at her sister and wondered when she'd gotten so grown up. "Lucy? Did you hear me? What are you doing in here?"

"Just looking around. What are you doing?" The shrug was so typically Cybill. "The cook asked me what we wanted for dinner, and I told her we've not decided. I don't want to keep him waiting too long. Are you hungry?"

"Not really. I mean, I want to eat, but not here. I don't know. It feels as if we should be celebrating or something. Don't you think? With Ian. He's my brother now." Lucy said she knew that. "He's a nice man. I really like him. I know you don't, but it's going to be — "

"I never said I didn't like him, Cybill. I just don't know him. You have to admit, it's only been a few days since we met him. I mean, in that little bit of time, I've had my arm hurt, we're no longer living in a van, Jilly has been operated on, we're in this mammoth of a house. And this one is the hardest to believe — I'm married. I think with all this going on, at the same time, we can at least be conscious of the fact that I'm a little stressed out." Cybill told her how sorry she was. "I don't want you to think you can't voice how you feel. But I do want you to think about how I'm feeling, all right?"

"Yes. I guess I can be sort of pushy. But I have to tell you, Lucy, this is the safest I've felt in a long time. I know you do as well." Lucy told her sister she did feel safe here. "Good. How about this? We can pick up something to eat — get a bunch of those little boxes of Chinese food — and take it in to eat with Jilly. You call Ian and see if he wants to join us. It'll be our first meal as a family. Whatcha think?"

"I'll ask, but don't get your hopes up too much. He's a busy man, and does work."

She realized she knew he made computers and such, but nothing much more than that. Picking up her new cell phone, she pushed the preset she was sure was his. As soon as Demi answered, she told her she was sorry.

"Don't be. I should have said I was answering Ian's phone. He's doing a job for me at the moment." Lucy told her what Cybill wanted to do. "What a wonderful idea. You tell your sister he'll be there with bells on. I'll order for you, so you have enough food, and have it delivered to you. Do you have a car to get there?"

"I'm to understand Ian left us a car to use." Demi told her she'd send a car to take them to the hospital. "I don't want to put you out. We can drive."

"You're not putting me out at all. We're in for the night after Ian leaves here. Being nearly ready to pop, it's tiring to be up past nine in the evening. I'm secretly hoping the baby comes sooner rather than later. I'm tired of being hugely pregnant and unable to stay awake once I sit for any longer than ten seconds." They both laughed. "I'll do this because I want to make up for having your new hubby here instead of where you are. I know you're taking things slowly, but he should at least sleep there. Just in case that uncle of yours comes around. By the way, did I mention that Meadow spoke to him today? It was a hoot for her. I'll tell you about it tomorrow."

"All right. But why would she want to speak to him at all?" Demi told her what was said to him and how he thought it had been a dream. "So, you've taken his money?"

"No. I took you and your sisters' money from him and gave it back to you. It's being funneled through a couple of banks now. You'll be notified when you have to go down and sign the paperwork for you to use it. I didn't assume you were sharing with Ian. I thought that was good of me." Again, they both laughed. "You'll need to sign off on paperwork when you get to the bank anyway. Ian signed the house over to you. Before you get all upset over that, you should know we're doing it like this, so the courts will notice you have a home. Also, your uncle. I want him to be so confused when he gets here."

"Confused people tend to be mean ones, don't you think?" Demi told her they were also stupid. "I think Josh has been stupid most of his life. But if this works, I'm indebted to you."

"Nah. We're related now. If we don't stick together, then things go wrong. In this family, things tend to go wrong at the beginning, but they're easily fixed. You're a great addition to this family. With the girls, it's going to be nice having someone to talk to."

Ian came by and picked them up just as she was hanging up the phone from talking to Demi. His car wasn't really big enough for the three of them, and he said he'd have to look for a new one. That his brother worked at a car dealership, and he'd get a nice discount from him.

"I don't know why I said that. None of us have ever asked for the discount. It's for family. As big as our families are getting, that could be a bad thing for his place." Lucy asked him what he'd do with this car. "I was going to talk to you about that. I thought that once Jilly starts driving, she'd use it to take herself and Cybill to class. If it's all right with you."

"That's what I was thinking too. She's going to need something, and I'd rather she had a newer car that she can rely on rather than a beater that needs to be repaired all the time." Lucy looked at her sister in the back seat when she laughed. "You don't think she'd like this car?"

"She'd love it. I think it's funny that you think she's going to want to take me anywhere. I don't know if you noticed this or not, but Jilly likes boys, and having her little sister around isn't going to be a good thing." Ian laughed, and Lucy frowned. "It's all right, Lucy. I don't mind riding the bus. I'm actually looking forward to going back to school. It's been a long time, and I only hope I can catch up to where the rest of the class is now."

"I never thought about you being behind." Ian told her there were all kinds of classes she could catch up with online. "I might have to look into that. Cybill has already figured out what she wants in her room. I hope it's all right that I've ordered it."

Lucy was still nervous about things like ordering and having money. It had only been about thirteen months since their parents had died, and most of that time had been spent by them living on the streets.

Jilly was sitting in a chair when they arrived. Her color was good, Lucy thought. She also told them she didn't have a headache anymore, and that she had slept like a log. Lucy asked if the doctor had told her what had happened.

Almost as if they'd summoned him, the surgeon walked into the room. He had been told they were headed in and came in to talk to them about what he'd found during surgery. Ian took her hand into his as the doctor spoke. It was just the kind of security she needed right then.

"The bullet, by how it was in her skull, looked to me like she'd been the victim of a freak accident. We try to get the word out that when firing a gun into the air, the bullet will still have to come back to earth, but I don't think people think beyond having a little fun. From the trajectory, I'd said that is exactly what happened." Ian asked about the second wound. "The same thing, I believe. Only it had been slowing down a lot sooner than the one that had embedded itself in Jilly's head. It doesn't happen all that much, but as I said, the bullet fired upwards has to come down at some point. Jilly just happened to be there when it came down."

Relieved that it wasn't someone trying to kill her, Lucy hugged her sister. All kinds of things had been racing through her mind about it. Had her uncle tried to kill her? Was someone else out to get them? She was so glad it was just as simple as it sounded. Hugging her again, Lucy told her sisters how much she loved them.

The food arrived not long after the doctor left. As bags of it were set on the extra rolling table that had been brought in, Lucy wondered who the hell Demi thought she was feeding. It looked to her like she'd ordered all the menu.

Not only was there so much food, but there were paper plates and napkins — plasticware too. There were bottles of water, along with tea. And a huge thermos of hot water and tea bags so they could enjoy a nice cup of hot tea later. As they were laying it all out, reading the names of each thing as they did, the nurse came in to thank them for the abundance of food for the staff.

"Demi McCray did all this. I'm sure you all know her." The nurse said they knew all the McCrays. She'd actually gone to school with Lucian. "I'm just getting to know them all. Ian and I were married earlier today. I love them all. They've taken such good care of us all."

"They would too. The new wing being put in for burn victims is from their generosity. Then there is the funding drive they had this year for the kids that are having a hospital stay. They go home with a couple of games, as well as several books. It's been wonderful for a lot of families to have someone think of them. The large basket of food goes a long way when you have sick ones at home." Lucy glanced at Ian as he passed out food. "You've got yourself a good man, Lucy. Ian is the best of the best, I think. He's come in on his own time and fixed up the computers when they mess up. And he reprograms the smaller readers to suit the age of the child that might be using them. It's nice to have those to let the kids use as well."

The nurse thanked them again and went back to the desk. Ian piled his plate full of a little of this and that. When he sat down, he asked the girls if they liked football. Their response was quite loud and happy. Putting the pregame games on, the four of them watched television until nearly every bit of the food was gone. She'd have to remember that in the future. Ian could eat, and her sisters were a close second in the ability to pack away the food.

She was nearly asleep on the way home. It was nice having her belly full, being warm, and knowing they were all safe. As they made their way up to the front door, Lucy asked Ian where he was staying. He told her that until they were able to put beds in the bedrooms, he was sleeping at his mom's.

Lucy felt guilty about that. It was his home, after all. But he assured her it was fun because he was getting to hang out with his mom during jam making season. Laughing with her, Ian kissed her on the cheek and left her there.

"I'll come by in the morning so we can fill out the rest of the rooms. I know Cybill has her things coming, but she might find something she enjoys more. Plus, we get to pick up Jilly.

We'll make it a family day for the four of us." Waving bye to them both, Ian told Cybill to behave, and then he drove off.

Lucy stood there for several minutes after he was gone. When she spied the rocker on the front porch, she made her way to it to just enjoy the night sounds. Also, she needed to think. Things weren't really overwhelming her now. Nor was she upset any longer that she'd married Ian.

He really was a nice man. Polite and generous. He also had a great sense of humor. When there was a question put to him from her sisters, he answered them without talking down to them. And he was honest to a fault. All his family was. It startled her when Cybill had asked a question, and it was answered so truthfully it even scared Cybill for a moment.

"Bears are bears. So if you see one of us out, you don't run, you don't scream or make any sudden moves. They protect all of us when necessary. When we get Jilly home, we'll all shift so we can all know your scents. Just be careful around them. They're dangerous without meaning to be."

Of course, Cybill couldn't wait to meet up with one of them now.

Chapter 4

Ian was having the time of his life. Who would have thought that spending the day with three women would have him laughing so hard he hurt from it? Although he was very careful not to let them see him laughing, he did let a little out once in a while that would get him evil looks. But he loved them all.

"I don't know why you think this is funny. It's stressful. You'd think they'd never had a bedroom suit before. It's just pick one, and we can move on." He didn't point out to Lucy that she'd yet to get one for their bedroom. Ian thought he might live a little longer if he didn't. "I should just make them sleep on the floor and be done with the lot of them."

"Have you decided what you want to do with your other home?" She turned and looked at him so quickly he was sure she was going to hurt him. Even his bear curled up. "I was only asking because if they wanted to wait on that stuff, we could just get something small for now."

"I don't have much in my parents' house. I'd already moved out a few years before." She looked at the linens on a long tall shelf beside them. "I don't even know if I'd want anything from the house. Uncle Josh, he's spoiled it all for me. Maybe I should bring it up to the others."

When she walked away, he wandered over to the living room things. He'd been wanting more than just a single couch in the room. The fireplace was an added bonus for him when winter rolled in. Not that he was normally chilled, but it was really nice to have a fire in the thing.

He was staring at one of the recliners, wondering if it was as uncomfortable as it looked, when someone walked up behind him. They touched him—not hard, but enough for Ian to know that he was there. From the scent of him, he knew he didn't know him. Ian turned toward him slowly.

"Hello, Ian. I've been looking for you." Ian only tipped his head at the man but said nothing. "Where is she? I need to talk to her right now."

"And who is it you need to speak to? Whoever it is, you should probably understand that approaching any of the women in my family as you just did me will get you killed." The man asked if he was threatening him. "No. Just a heads up. Who is it you're looking for?"

"Demi McCray. She's been avoiding me. I really have to talk to her." Reaching out to Demi, he told her what was going on. She, of course, had plenty to say about someone she was avoiding. "I want you to call her. Right now. Before I have to shoot you full of holes right here in front of your family. Nice one, by the way."

"Thanks." He looked to where his wife and her sisters were and wished now that he'd warned Lucy he could talk to her. Telling her by their link to stay back, she gathered up the other two and made their way in the opposite direction from where he and the man were standing. "I don't know why you'd think I carry Demi around in my pocket, but she's not here. Nor do I have any idea where she is."

"You all are stuck up each other's ass all the time. Just pull out your phone slowly and call her."

Ian saw the gun then. Well, the man made a big deal of showing it to him. The only problem was, he had it in the top of his pants instead of in his hand. Ian pulled out his phone but didn't bother calling anyone on it. He handed it to the man. Ian thought he'd have fingerprints on it if the man were to kill him, which was looking more likely every second.

"You're to call her. Just fucking do as you're told." He saw Lucian as he moved around them to where Lucy had gone. Ian hadn't seen Demi as yet. He asked her where she was.

We're here in the shopping center with you guys. To be honest, we've seen you here three times, but have been avoiding you so you could enjoy your shopping trip. I'm here for a baby bed. Don't even ask about the one we already had. He was going to ask his brother about it later. It was just too good not to know that she'd made him want more information. *There you are. Lucian is with Lucy and the girls. Has he told you what he wanted?*

Just you. And he has a gun. So far, all he's said is that we're up each other's ass. Why would someone say that to me? Anyway, I'm all right so long as he keeps the gun in his pants.

Demi made her way to them, slowly looking around to make sure there wasn't anyone else close by who might be caught in the crossfire if there was any. Ian turned back to the recliner, hoping to distract the man from looking around and seeing Demi.

"Do you think this chair is ugly? The reason I ask is, I think the pattern on it is a little sickening. Not to mention, it's puffy in places I'd think—" The man asked him what the fuck he was talking about. "The chair. Is it ugly? Or would you think it's one of those pieces that goes with everything? It is colorful, isn't it?"

"Are you daft? I told you to get Demi here." Ian talked more about the chair and the colors on it until the man pulled out his gun and pushed it into his belly. "Do I have your full attention now, fuck tard? Call Demi and get her here, right the fuck now."

Ian was never so glad to see someone as he was Demi. Even the fact that she had a gun rammed up against the head of the man in front of him didn't faze him. When she told him to take the gun, he did so without arguing about how much he hated them.

"What the hell do you want with me? I'm sick to fucking death of people coming up on my family and trying to get shit from them when the easier route is to contact me. You'd better have a fucking good reason for me not to kill you right where you stand." The man said he had a deal for her. "Deal? You're willing to risk your life for a fucking deal? You really are stupid, aren't you?"

"It's a good deal. I've been told you were looking for businesses to bring to town. Well, I have the deal of all deals for you." She told him she wasn't interested. "But you can make a lot of money off this. We both can."

"Nope. Not the least bit interested in anything you have to say to me. For starters, coming up on my family with a gun will get you disqualified right off the bat. Secondly — well, I just don't fucking like the way you do business." The man turned, and Demi allowed it. "You're going to get yourself dead if you don't get the hell away from me and mine right now."

"You're going to turn down the deal of a lifetime." She said she had before and it didn't bother her. "I thought for sure you were going to be willing and able to get this started. Perhaps what I've heard is true about you. You got yourself knocked up, and now you don't have the brains to know anything anymore."

Demi looked at Ian. "Do you believe this shit? He's actually insulting me when he wants to tell me about the deal of the century." The man said it was a lifetime deal. "Oh, pardon me, the deal of a lifetime. I wonder if he realizes first impressions are what gets you in the door."

"It certainly doesn't look like he knows much of anything." Ian laughed and asked Demi if she and Lucian wanted to have dinner with them. "My treat. I'm suddenly very happy that you're related to me. And I've only just realized that I want that ugly chair. I think it's sexy now."

"I don't know if a chair could be considered sexy, Ian. But hey, whatever floats your turds." She smiled at him. "By the way, I like the chair. It's ugly in a sort of — "

"The police are here." Lucian tapped him on the shoulder as a way of greeting as he continued. "You just had to be here today, didn't you? I had great plans for today. Dinner with my wife. A nice shopping trip for a new bed."

"I thought you had one." The man was arrested, and Lucian told him about the bed. "You thought you could put a piece of furniture together that you're going to be putting your infant in without reading the instructions. Remind me again what sort of education you have?"

"Hey, it was in several languages, and I got caught up in the pictures." Lucy and the girls joined them. "Your new wife is mean. She told me that if you got hurt while I was with her, she'd castrate me. I don't believe for a moment she was joking either. Where do we find such violent women?"

"Lucky, I guess." Demi walked around with Lucy as he sat in the ugly chair. "I don't have any idea why, but this chair is sort of growing on me. What happened that brought the two of you into town? I don't believe for a minute that you messed up a baby bed for your own kid. What's going on?"

"The money that was being put into the accounts for Lucy and her sisters is there. Josh isn't happy. He went to the bank early this morning and found out that it's all gone. Not just that, but Meadow was able to figure out he had several safety deposit boxes filled with all kinds of jewelry and cash that he must have found around the house." Ian asked him if that was what brought them to town. "No. He's out cruising the streets looking for the girls. The welfare department, as well as the attorney's office that is writing the checks from the estate for the younger sisters, wants to talk to them. Josh, of course, isn't able to find them."

"You said the younger two. What is it that Lucy is supposed to be getting? Not that I care if she gets nothing at all, but I think you worded that the way you did because you know more." Lucian told him about the house and that it belonged to Lucy. "I don't think she wants it. At least that's what she said when we were talking. She thinks Josh being there and what he's doing to them has soured the house for her."

"If that's the case, then all the money from the sale of the house goes into the estate, and Lucy, if she decides to raise her sisters, gets a larger chunk of the cash. All three of them will share the insurance equally. That'll be close to three million apiece. Double that if the ruling on their deaths was accidental. Which I really don't know if a landslide is considered an accident or an act of God." Ian didn't know either. "Demi has been working on a couple of other things for them too. I guess there are a lot of things in a safety deposit box that Josh has been trying to get into since the parents died. Since he's never been put on any of the signature cards, they're keeping him away. Demi is afraid that if he gets a good attorney or at least a slick one, he'll get to that as well."

"Christ." Lucian told him that pretty much summed it up. When Jilly came and stood by the two of them, Ian smiled at her. Instead of smiling back, she asked him what was going on. "Nothing."

"Bullshit. And yes, I said that. What's going on? I can tell you're stressing about something. The little veins in your forehead are monstrous sized right now, and you're looking all pinched." He told her it was about her uncle. "What else is new. I also came over here to tell you that we're going to sell the house. The furniture inside of it, we want to be able to go through and decide on what we want. We've all decided we enjoy living with you in the house you have. It's never been tainted."

"If you'd rather have the furniture out of your old rooms, we can arrange that today. To be honest with you, I'm sort of sick of dicking around with Josh. You want it, then I will do everything within my power to get it for you." She said she did want her bedroom things. "All right. Lucian and I will figure this out, and you get with your sisters and see when would be a good time for them to go there. Even if we have to have Josh arrested right now, it's better than cowering in a corner waiting to see what he does next."

"Josh isn't at the house." Ian asked Lucian if he could arrange to have someone go there and change out the locks. "I can. Anything else? I'm willing and able to help you guys in any way I can. Legally or not."

"Nothing illegal right now. But we'll need someone there to keep an eye on things." Jilly said there were cars in the garage. "All right. We'll need a lot of people there to keep an eye on things. Also, we might as well have child services there, as well as an attorney that has had any dealings with the Jacksons."

Ian felt like he was finally doing something for his new family. It might all be a bust, and Josh could already be back at the house. But at least he was working to end this. He knew he'd sleep better if he knew all his family was getting their things back, and their uncle was getting what he deserved as well.

In forty minutes they were leaving the furniture store. Being armed with a list of things the three of them wanted, was making his job much easier. It wasn't going to be easy, he had no doubt about that. Something else was going to happen. But for now, he knew he was getting Josh out of their lives. At least the house anyway.

Josh hadn't shown up by the time they were in the driveway. There was a leap as well as a pack, friends of Demi's, wandering around the estate. Also, Meadow was there with her supercharged magic. Even his parents were there with several members of their bruin to help carry out things the girls wanted from the house. It couldn't have been better if he'd had weeks to plan this out.

The bedrooms were stripped first. Josh had been sleeping in the master bedroom, so no one bothered going in there until Melody suggested tearing the bed down in the event that Josh got in. That way, he'd have no bed unless he was willing to put it back together. Lucy went through her parents' things and found a lot of their jewelry missing. Cybill found the will that had been doctored.

"He actually thought this would work." Jilly pointed out that it had so far. "I guess. But look here. He misspelled two words in the first part of it. Why hasn't anyone noticed that before now?"

"Because, my dear, you're fresh at looking at it. People who read wills all the time are so used to seeing what it's supposed to say that they're jaded when it comes to actually reading the words." Melody took the will from Cybill and handed it to Ian. "You need to call the police and tell them what you've found here. I'll have Shoe bring over the original will, the one we found on file, and compare notes. He'll get to the bottom of this part."

Lucy asked if she could box up her parents' clothing and such when Mr. Shoe, Demi and Lucian's attorney, showed up. He was a dapper little man, and Ian really enjoyed talking to him. He hugged Demi and turned to speak to Lucy. "I'd wait to have pictures taken of it first. Just to be on the safe side. It's all yours legally, but just so you can show Josh that you've not done anything behind anyone's back about things." She agreed with Mr. Shoe. "However, the things in the girls' bedrooms, it can be packed up and taken away. It has always belonged to them."

It didn't take them long to get the beds into one of the trucks, as well as the other pieces from their bedrooms. With shifters there to help, the dressers didn't need to be unpacked. They were just picked up and put on the truck with the rest of the things.

It was all going very smoothly, then Josh showed up. The police, there already to make sure everything taken out of the house was actually a part of the estate, kept out of sight until they were called for. The way Josh was arguing with his nieces, Ian didn't think it was going to be very long until someone yelled for help.

~*~

Lucy had to keep telling herself not to hit him. It was

tempting. She wanted to sock him in the nose so badly she had to keep clenching and unclenching her fist so she wouldn't. He asked her again why she'd left the house in the first place.

"You forced us out. Not to mention, you dropped us off at the mall like we were a bunch of teenagers that were going to meet their friends." Josh only shook his head. "I want you to get out of my home. And off the property. I've had enough of you for one lifetime."

"Hold on a minute here. I'm the one taking care of the estate of my long lost brother. You're under my care." Lucy told him she was twenty-two years old. "Okay, so not you. But I am to care for the other two. You just have to sign the insurance over to me, as per your dad's will, so I can keep them living here without any trouble."

"No. I'm not signing anything over to you. You have no rights to anything my parents left us." He said he had the will. "You have one you fixed up so you'd have the money. You didn't get that either, did you? I'm happy to tell you it's been moved into an account so we can use it."

"You took my money? How the hell did you figure that out? Damn it, Mary, that money was mine for my golden years." She told him her name was Lucy. Then told him his golden years were going to be spent in prison. "No, that's not going to happen either. Not that it matters anyway, whatever your name is. You're going to do as you're told, or I'm going to call the police on you. I've tried to be nice, but now that you're here, I've decided you're much too old for me to be caring for anyway."

"What?" Josh said she was too old for him to care for.

"Why do you think I'm here, Josh? To have an argument with you? No. I'm here to get what I want from our home. Once you're arrested, we're going to put the house on the market and do what Mom and Dad wanted us to do with the real will. Not the one you have."

"This is the real will." She pointed out what Cybill had shown her. "So? Your dad had a stupid attorney. Besides, where did you get yours? I got this one from the safe."

"No, you didn't. But I got mine at the county courthouse. It was filed along with my parents' deed to the house. I'm also making a list of things that have been taken." Josh told her he'd not taken a single item from her mother's jewelry box. "I never said anything about jewelry, Josh. But now that you have, where are her diamond earrings? The brooch that was my grandmas? There are a few more pieces of Dad's that I can't find. Like the pocket watch and his tie clasps."

"You're blowing this all out of whack, Lucy. Let's just go inside and talk this over like adults. Then when we're finished up, you can go your way, and I can continue living here while caring for my niece and nephew."

"They're both girls, and no, you're not." He looked around like he was looking for someone to help him out. Lucy had had enough and asked Ian to get the police for her. "In the event you took more than the jewelry, I'm going to press charges against you for a lot of things that are missing, as well as you trying to get us killed by dropping us off when we should have been able to live here."

"Lucy, you're looking at this all wrong. I'm your own living relative. You need me." She said she had a husband

and his entire family to depend on. "You're married? I don't remember anyone asking me for your hand. I'm sure you're only telling me this so you can get more out of my estate planning here."

"Blow it out your ass." She was feeling better until he told her she was going to prison for this. "Me? No, you have that all wrong too. I'm not going anywhere, you are."

She wanted Ian with her. To lean on him while she tried to fix what was going on. When he came back, wrapping his arm around her waist, Lucy felt strong enough to take on the world. As soon as Josh was cuffed and being led to the cruiser, she looked at the house once again.

"I can't live here. Not ever." Ian told her he was there for her in whatever she decided. "I'm not sure selling it is a good idea. What if one of my sisters wants it when they get married? Or we can sell it for them to be able to put money down on one they want. I don't know, but selling it right now just doesn't seem right."

"I like that as a plan. Also, you can take your time now in going through things and seeing what it is you want to keep." She nodded, but still didn't think she wanted much more than the things she had for her sisters. "I hope you don't mind, but I had some of the people here go through the refrigerator and cabinets to take out the food. I didn't think you'd want to leave it until you come back. I don't think Josh is coming back for some time."

"That's the best news I've had all day." She turned and leaned her back to his chest as she watched her sisters gathering things up and putting them on the front porch to be taken to Ian's home. "Are you sure you don't mind them living with us? I mean, they've been really good so far, but I keep waiting for the other shoe to drop with them. They argue like it's their job."

"I have five brothers, remember." She laughed. "Yes, I love having them there. I don't know how good I'm going to do with them dating, but for now, I think having them around is fun. They sure can spice up things when they want to, can't they?"

"Yes. They're very good at that." Cybill came out of the house with an armload of what appeared to be picture frames. "I'd better go see what she's doing now. I think they do not realize we can and will come back, and are taking things from the house like protesters at a bad call on a Friday night football game."

He was still laughing as she made her way across the yard. There were little touches here that her mom had done when she'd been alive. The perennials that were in full bloom despite the cooler weather. The wagon wheel that held up the roses Dad had planted for her. Little things like that. She came up on Cybill as she was putting some of the things from Dad's desk into another box.

"I want Dad's desk." Lucy said it would have to be a decision she and Jilly came to. "She told me I could have it so long as she got to take Mom's fainting chair. I think I'm getting the better end, but she really loves that chair."

"Okay. But once it leaves here and it's in the house, no more trade backs. Okay?" Cybill told her how Dad had shown her how to write her name sitting with her at this desk. She'd never part with it. "I think Mom showed Jilly how to repair the needlepoint on the chair she wants too. All right. But how about we do this. We mark the things we want with paper, and when we come back here with more trucks, we can move out what we want and sell off the rest."

Jilly said she was fine with that, but she didn't want to live here. Lucy said she didn't either. They both looked at Cybill. She just stared at the house before looking at the two of them.

"I have a lot of memories here. Too many of them to deal with in one day. I'm going to think about the things I want and make sound decisions about them. But as for the house, no, I don't want to live here either. Not even with Ian and his family close by. Mom and Dad, they loved this house. But to me, it was always so...I don't know. Not cold, but them. Does that make sense?" Jilly said that was what she thought too. The house wasn't theirs. "Yes, that's it. It's not a family house either. When I get married, I want a family house. Bright with lights and shiny floors. Like Ian's house. All the windows in his home make me feel like the sun is shining just for me."

Ian came up just as they were talking about his home, and he kissed both her sisters on their cheeks. It was a good time for them, with family around them and Josh out of their hair. There were things they all three had to deal with yet, but it was getting easier every day to think about. Ian did that for them, he and his family. They'd brought them to their home and made them family. Lucy didn't think she'd been a part of a family for a long time.

Her parents had been good people. They worked hard and kept them safe. But they weren't huggers, she only just realized. They were standoffish, sort of cold. If one of them did something good in school, they took them out to dinner rather than hang things on the fridge. Cindy, Ian's mom, still had things on her fridge from when the boys were smaller.

Lucy wanted that too. To have a large family that gathered together in times of fun and need. She wanted to be able to take her sisters shopping, just to show them that girls could have fun too. Even inviting Demi and the other two women with them would be something she was going to do. Anything and everything to be a unit. Something she only just realized she wanted.

Lucy turned to Ian. "I want lots of children with you." He told her he'd like that too. "Good. I want huge, overly done holidays. Vacations in a camper so we can hang out together. Trips to museums and libraries. I'd like to be a member of clubs so I can have friends. True friends, not the kind my parents had."

"I love that idea, as well. Lucy, I do love you." She looked at his eyes and could see it there. He really did love her. She laid her head on his chest and told him she was beginning to fall in love with him too. "I'm so glad you came into my life. I plan to show you how glad I am about it every minute of every day. I love your sisters and how they're enriching our lives as well. Lucy McCray, I'll never for as long as I live love anyone as much as I do you right now. Tomorrow it will be more love for you, as it will be every day we're together."

She kissed him then. Holding his body to hers, she gave as good as she got from him. Lucy was in love with Ian, she realized. Loved him so much that her heart seemed too small to hold it all. She would tell him too. Tell him every day that she loved him just as much as he did her. Life, Lucy came to realize, was never going to be as good as it was with Ian in her heart.

Chapter 5

Jilly wasn't sure what she'd expected, but the bears in front of her were bigger than any she'd seen at the zoo. Not only that, usually there were only one or two of them. There were six of the big monsters here. They weren't the warm and cuddly kind either like she'd had stuffed on her bed when she was a child.

"Can I touch you?" Jilly started to reach for Cybill. Why on earth would anyone want to touch these things? When the one in front of her put out his paw, she could see that his claws were as long as any knife she'd seen in their kitchen. "You're Ian, aren't you? I think I can tell that because of the mark you have on your ear. Did you know you have a small white place of fur there?"

Grandpa McCray came and sat with them. He told them he was there to tell them what the bears were telling them. Then he mentioned that if they let the bears take just a little of their blood, they'd be able to talk to them too. Jilly put both her hands under her butt and shook her head.

"You don't have to, child. They'd not ever take something you're not willing to give them. Here, Cybill. You let me put a little cut here on your finger, and that'll be all Ian needs to speak to you."

The blood welted up on her sister's finger, and Ian, the bear, licked it clean. Cybill giggled.

"He said to tell you he'd never hurt you. He'd rather die than to hurt any of us. I believe him, Jilly. And it didn't hurt me at all to have Grandpa McCray cut me just a little." Shaking her head no, Jilly watched as the other bears played and chased one another around the yard. Ian went to join them. "You're a big baby."

"Did he say that?" Cybill said he'd told her Jilly could do as she wished, it was her that said she was a baby. "I'm not a baby, Cybill. Just look at them. They must weigh a ton each."

"Not quite that much, I'm afraid. Not that it matters if you're a tad afraid of them, but they only weigh about five hundred pounds each. Still, that's pretty big." She told Grandpa McCray she wasn't afraid of them. "I know that, sweetie. They just take some getting used to. That's all I meant. Why, any one of them would die for any of us. Even me, being a bear myself, they'd still protect me. Yes, they're large but about as sweet as my lady wife is."

Jilly wasn't going to allow anyone to think she was afraid. Getting up, she approached the bears at play and stood still when they stopped to look at her. The biggest one, she just knew it was going to be Ian, moved toward her and rubbed his large head against her arm. Petting him seemed to be just what he wanted.

"That there is Lucian. He's bigger on account 'a him being the oldest. Ian is right behind him. If you let Lucian there have a taste of your blood, they'll all know your scent and how to find you." Jilly wasn't sure this was such a good idea once she was standing with them. "Go on, Jilly. I promise you, not a single one will harm you."

Putting out her hand, she was embarrassed that it was shaking. But none of them seemed to care. When Lucian put his mouth over her finger, she felt the immediate pain, then nothing. He bowed before her like she was some sort of queen, then he moved away. Ian came to stand closer to her.

You're very brave in letting Lucian do that. He's really impressed. She looked at Ian as he spoke to her. *I want you to know that if you were ever to get away from us, any of us can find you. You can also speak to your sisters, as well as the other women. Just think of them, whoever you want to talk to, and they'll be able to answer you. Until you get used to whose voices you're hearing, ask them if you don't know.*

"Is that important? That I'm able to speak to all of you?" He told her it was very important. They got a signal better than a cell phone. "When you come to save me or whatever, will you be a bear or a person?"

It would depend greatly on the reason why you need us. But we can speak to you and answer you in either form. However, finding you if you don't know where you are is easier as a bear because bears have a better sense of smell than humans. She told him she was afraid Josh was going to hurt them. *He might try. But I don't plan on allowing him to touch any of you.*

"And if he does? If, for whatever reason, he gets to us and takes or hurts us, what will you do to him?" Ian told her he'd be dead. "You'd do that?"

Yes.

When he didn't say anything more, she nodded and sat down next to her sister again. Watching the guys playing around, Jilly thought of what would happen if her uncle came after any of them. She knew Ian would do just what he said he'd do. He'd kill him without a second thought. Jilly almost felt sorry for her uncle. Almost.

He'd hurt them. Though none of them were permanently hurt or scarred, he still threw them away like they were nothing more than an unwanted sheet of paper. He took what belonged to them. Didn't make sure they were well fed or even warm. What sort of person did that to his own flesh and blood? Jilly decided it was something she'd never do. She'd tell her children daily that she loved them.

Her parents hadn't done that. Jilly couldn't remember a time when they all sat around the kitchen table and talked and laughed together. She'd done that very thing this morning with Ian and her sisters. Even the cook had laughed with them, telling them stories of Ian when he was a small boy.

Birthdays, she remembered, weren't planned. A gift would show up on their bed. There would be a card with money in it. One year, just before they died, they'd forgotten Cybill's birthday altogether. And when she had told them about it, they'd acted as if it wasn't all that big of a deal. It had been to her sister.

Jilly began to remember other things like that. While her parents weren't terrible people, they certainly weren't loving. No hugs were given in the event they had to meet someone later.

Her parents also argued, loudly at times. No blood was shed. They never spoke of divorce. As far as Jilly could remember, they never fought with them around. She only ever heard it from their bedroom or Dad's office. Mostly it was about spending. Her mom, she remembered, loved expensive jewelry and evening gowns. Something that neither her nor her sisters seemed to have gotten from the house. She did wonder what had happened to the few pieces she remembered but dismissed it. Like she'd be able to ever wear something that her mother had worn.

Dad had been short of stature. She hadn't realized it until she began to hang around the McCray men. All of them were taller than six feet. Jilly thought her dad had only been about five foot six or seven. Certainly not any more than that. He had also been very slim — too thin, she thought. But not her mom.

Mom was taller than Dad had been, but not by much. She was forever on a diet, it seemed. Something that would have her lose weight for a while, then she'd plump back up. Jilly only just realized her mom would go out and buy long gowns at those times — when her body was at the weight she wanted it to be. Which wasn't all that often.

"Did you hear me?" She shook her head at Cybill. "I asked if you wanted to get in the pool. The others are gone now — they have to get some work done. Did you know that Ian makes computers? I'm going to ask for one for Christmas."

"I'll go up and change and meet you here in a few minutes." Jilly stood up and thought she must have been thinking very hard if she missed her sister changing into her suit already.

Laughing at herself, Jilly made her way up to her room, a room that was becoming something she loved. There had been no stipulations on how they decorated their room, nor on what sort of furniture they had in it. It was their space, both Ian and Lucy had told her and Cybill, but to remember that the room couldn't change again for a year. That seemed to her not too long of a time frame. However, when she started looking at furniture and how she wanted it to look, she made herself remember that rule over and over.

Deciding to go with just plain white walls in her room made it seem like she could do anything else with colorful furniture. It hadn't turned out the way she had thought it would. Colorful prints at the store looked pretty cool to her, but thinking about having to wake up to the large bright blots of color made her rethink it all.

Keeping the walls white had been a good choice. She liked the freshness of it, the way it seemed like a new day—a clean slate, so to speak. Jilly looked at things for her room that would be just as fresh to her. A good way to wake up in the morning and have a wonderful morning. Deciding on the light oak furniture as well as a pretty tiny print on her bedspread and curtains looked just exactly like she wanted it to look when she was finished. Then Demi came over and gave both her and Cybill a painting.

Jilly hadn't asked if it was a real piece of art. She could see the name of the most famous painter she'd ever heard of in the corner. The flowers were just the right colors of blue, the sky, another shade of the hue. Knowing just what she wanted after that, Jilly picked out a shade of blue that didn't take away from the painting, but she thought it brought it all together. Her room, she thought, was both calming and fresh. The colors, even though there weren't that many, made her smile every time she entered or left her room. Cybill asked for her help to do the same to her room, and they both had rooms that not only did they love, but were all theirs.

The pool was perfect. As they played in the water, Jilly thought of something else. Instead of letting it simmer in her head, she asked Cybill about it. They'd had a pool at their other home. Did she remember ever using it?

"Now that you mention it, I don't remember ever using it. It was there for Mom and Dad's parties, but no one seemed to want to get in and have some fun." Cybill got out and sat on the edge of the pool to talk to her. "I've been comparing our life with Ian and Lucy to Mom and Dad too. They didn't do much, did they?"

"You mean like vacations and such?" Cybill said out to dinner with them. "Yeah, we didn't do that either. Unless it was some kind of business thing. Then we had to sit quietly and not speak to anyone unless they spoke to us first. But I loved them. You know?"

"I did too. I just never thought about how strict they were until now. But that's not right either. It's how they were never there, even when they were home." Cybill looked around at the woods they were situated in, at the pool house, and the greenhouse too. Jilly asked her what she was thinking about. "I don't know. I'm just letting thoughts go around and around in my head. Like the day Mom and Dad left on the trip that got them killed. Neither one of them said goodbye. If I'd not seen the car leaving when they left, I doubt we would have even missed them for a few days. They were forever leaving without saying anything. That's really sad, don't you think?"

"I didn't mean to make you sad, Cybill. I was just thinking to myself." Cybill said she'd been thinking too. "Is it because of the McCrays? I think Lucy is different now too. I mean, doesn't she look like she's going to burst with happiness? I know she's having a blast with the other women. I am too. They're not related to us at all, but I still call them my aunts. I noticed you did that as well."

"They make you just feel. Like everything. The other day I was on the deck just watching the trees when I realized what I was doing. I swear to you, Jilly, they were singing to me. I mentioned that to Grandma Cindy, and she told me they more than likely were. All of earth will speak to you if you're quiet enough to listen." Cybill laughed. "She wasn't even scolding me to be quiet then either. She meant it."

"Hey, girls." Jilly was so happy to see Lucy that she felt her face stretch into a huge smile. She looked better too—all of them did now that they were eating better and sleeping in a real bed. "You don't have to go with me, but I'm headed to the bakery. I'm supposed to see what sort of ingredients I'll need to order, as well as any equipment. The other women will be there too. You want to go? I'll treat you to lunch."

Both she and Cybill scrambled to get ready to go. Not that having lunch with their sister was the best part of it for her. Jilly would have gone anyway. But to be in the bakery while they were working on it made her want to grab up a tool and work too. Jilly wanted to make things with her hands so badly that she shook whenever she was near things like that.

Putting on her most casual clothing, hoping against hope that she'd be able to drive a nail in or something equally fun, she was downstairs waiting when Cybill joined them. She, of course, was dressed in a summer dress and sandals. Unlike her, Cybill enjoyed dresses. Jilly wanted to be pretty but comfy. Just like her big sister.

~*~

Ian worked on the computer while keeping an eye on his family. Mostly it was Jilly. She seemed to be itching to get herself into trouble. He wasn't worried about her getting hurt with the things she would pick up, but he knew she was going to convince one of the workers to allow her to use the nail gun — he just knew it. As soon as the thought entered his mind, Jilly was holding the gun to the wall with help.

"It's got a little kick, so you have to put all your weight against it to make sure you don't misfire." She nodded, pulling on the safety glasses as she listened. "Now, we're shifters, so we have a little more muscle than you might have, so when you pull the trigger, make sure you only pop it once. More than that, and we'll have to pull the second nail out."

He watched her do it and realized she'd done a good job of it. Keeping an eye on Cybill was easier. She had absolutely no desire at all to get dirty. It was kinda cute, really, how she was able to avoid touching anything with either the dress she had on or her hands. Jilly was already sporting a fine sheen of sweat and dirt on her hands.

Lucy was going over the list of equipment that had been left at the bakery when Demi purchased it. Lucy and Melody were going to be partners in the bakery. Lucy was going to do the baking, and Melody the cook for things like soup and sandwiches. He thought it was going to be very busy once they were opened. Even Lucian expressed a desire to be the taste tester for all the things they made.

"I've made some different kinds of breads to see what it is you wanted me to make." Melody told her she wanted them all. "You've not even tasted them. For all you know they could be crap."

"No. I can smell them. If that's the way crap smells, then we should put a bow on it and put it on the market too." Cybill made a gagging sound. "Come here, kid. You need to pull out some of the paper plates so we can slice this up and have everyone trying them."

Cybill did it in her most dainty way. Jilly was still using the nail gun on the wall while two men put up drywall they were using. The difference between the two girls was vast, and funny to him. Ian made his way to the sample table too. Even though he'd already had several slices of the bread at home, he was never going to pass up more of it. Not if he could help it.

The brown bread was his favorite. He did understand it might not be everyone's cup of tea. Also, with it being so sweet, to him at least, he could see where someone might not want it as a sandwich bread. He thought ham on the bread would be just the thing.

With several slices of bread on his plate, he went back to the computer. Mom came in then, sad that she'd missed the tasting, and offered up some of her jam for next time. Everyone turned to him, knowing he had some stashed under his work station.

Sharing his bread was harder than he thought it should have been. Perhaps because he ended up with less than a slice of the yummy treat when he'd had as many as four full slices on his plate. His wife called him selfish, and his mom told him to behave. He smiled at them both as he shoved the piece in his mouth with some of his mom's black raspberry jam spread out all over it.

Jilly asked to hang around with him and the workers while the others went to buy some of the supplies still needed. The Gathering Place was set to open in a week, and everyone around town was excited. He was too. The things that Lucy had been making at home for them was going to make the entire town overweight. Even her things like small cookies were so sinfully good that he could and would eat all of them without someone taking them from him.

"Do you think I could work with the construction company?" Ian told Jilly she'd have to ask Demi. They all worked for her. "Do you think she'd have a problem with me working? I mean, I am a girl and all."

"First of all, so what if you're a girl? Do you have it in your head that girls can't do the same job as well as if not better than a man?" She smiled at him and told him no. "Good. Because if you say crap like that to Demi, you're going to be in deep shit. And I'm not going to bail you out of it. For that matter, I'd not say that to any of the women in this family. Even my mom would be upset with you for thinking along those lines. If you want to work in construction, then I'd work at it in the summer months. They'll be busier then, and you will be able to make some cash while you're at it. You take your test for your license soon, don't you?"

"Yes. Very soon. And since you gave me your car, I think my sister is happy too. She doesn't want me stranded someplace with a beater, she called it." Ian asked her about gas and insurance. "I don't know. I guess I just figured she'd give me that too. Or you would."

"I'll give you what you'll need for traveling back and forth to school and *help* you with insurance, but I'm not planning on paying for your party life." Jilly said she didn't have a party bone in her body. "Not yet. You're not out free with a car. Nope, not going to pay for that crap. You'll need a job, if for no other reason than so you can pay for things you'd like to have. Like, I don't know. I guess it would be girl stuff. Since I've never had a sister until recently, I haven't any idea what sort of gooey stuff a girl would want."

"Gooey stuff? I don't even know what that would be." She turned and looked at the work going on behind her. "Since I watched a company come and build shelves in my room, I've wanted to be a builder. Then as I got older, I realized it was much more than that. I wanted to learn to create. You know, make a design and then build it. It's been my deepest dream."

"Then I will go out of my way to make that happen for

you, Jilly." She looked at him, and he saw hope was there. It was tangible. Then it disappeared with the next blink of her eyes. "Who is it that told you that you couldn't do that? Your mom or dad?"

"Both."

Ian nodded. "You can count on me, Jilly. I will do as I promised, and make sure you can at least try and achieve this dream of yours."

"Seriously? What will Lucy say?" He said he'd talk to her. "She'll turn me down. I know she's nothing like our parents, thankfully, but she'll think it's manly too."

"No, I won't." Lucy came up behind Jilly and hugged her. "I forgot to measure the bins I'm going to be using. But I couldn't help but overhear what you want to do. Go for it, Jilly. There are just too many people out there in this world who think just because their gender isn't the usual one who does a job, they can't either. If Ian can't make it happen for you, then together, we will. Even if I have to make some heads roll. I want you to be whatever you want. Both you and Cybill. I'd not count on her working in construction, but you never know."

They were all three laughing as Lucy measured the six bins that had been found in the building. They'd been cleaned and sanitized, the seams sealed up and ready to be used. Ian thought they were perfect for the rest of the place. This place was beginning to look more like a bakery every day he was there.

"Would you like a job here?" Cybill asked suspiciously what the job would be. "Waiting tables. Taking orders on the phone. Ringing out customers. Things like that. No dishes, if that's what you're thinking. I don't know who was hired for that job, but the man is going to be living above the shop. He's going to be keeping an eye on things."

"I think I'd like that. I don't know how to do any of those things, but I think I can wing it." Lucy told her she'd have to wear an apron. "Good. I don't want to ruin my clothing. You won't fire me the first day, will you?"

Lucy and her sister talked about Cybill waiting tables as they left again. Jilly went back to work with the other men. She was the only female in the place, and the guys were falling all over themselves, trying to make sure she didn't get injured. Finally, just like her sister, she told them to all just do what they normally did. She wasn't a delicate flower as her sister was. After that, it was loud and dirty again. Jilly took it with stride and concentrated on making sure she learned the job she was doing.

So how old is Jilly? Ian had to smile. Of course, one of the women would have told Demi that Jilly wanted a job. He told her she'd be seventeen on Christmas Eve. *That's old enough so long as she doesn't cut off a finger or something. I mean, she's not supposed to be working in that sort of environment at all, but I think we can fudge that up for her. What do you think about her working around a bunch of jackasses?*

She can hold her own. Jilly has already told them to stop treating her like a wilting flower. Demi laughed. *For all I know, she might not enjoy this after a month or so. However, it has been a dream of hers to create, she told me. Not just that, but to design and create. I think she'd love it.*

I'd love to help her with her dream. She's a good kid. They both are. When she paused, he took his hand off the work he was doing. He wanted to devote his full attention to whatever she had to say to him. *He's made bail. I'm not sure how, but he's out and about. I know he's gone by the house to try and get in but didn't have any luck. I have a feeling he's going to be a problem that won't soon go away. Also, you asked me to look into him having anything to do with the deaths of their parents, and I didn't find anything. And you know me well enough to know that I looked.*

Cybill and Lucy are with you, so I'm not worried about them. And Jilly is here with me, so I'll keep a closer eye on her. What do you think he's going to do now? Other than try and hurt one of them to get back into the house? She said it was hard to say what he'd do. *I agree. I wish we knew a little more about him. I mean, is he a violent person? Does he carry a gun? Has he done any prison time?*

Violent? I haven't any idea. I would say he could be if pushed. All I could find on him was that he's spent a couple of nights in jail. Mostly for drunk driving on the lesser charges. Once because he was trespassing. Believe it or not, that wasn't his family calling them on him. Though I have run across the restraining order that Lucille, the girl's mother, had against him. I can't find the reason why, but there was one in place when she was killed. Ian asked her what she thought they should do now. *I really have no idea. I'd not flaunt being out and about when you see him. I think, and this is just me, I'd wait until he makes a move. He won't be long in doing that either. Josh got used to having money.*

His brother, Donald — do we know how their relationship was? I mean, obviously, his wife didn't care for her brother-in-law. Demi said they didn't get along at all from what she'd heard from other people. *I guess there will be a court hearing soon about him falsifying the will and stealing from the girls.*

Yes. I'm pushing for it to be sooner rather than later. She laughed. *Your little wife is a hellion. Someone cut us off, and she's about ready to jump from the car and do him in. I'd not mess with her if I were a bad guy. I think she's had a taste of being safe, and she doesn't want anything to take that away from her. Oh, your adoption paperwork has been finalized. All the girls have to do is sign that they weren't forced to have you as their father.*

He was a dad. It hit him every time someone brought it up. After Demi told him where they were, they closed the connection. Keeping an eye on Jilly, he was happy to see that she'd progressed from using the nail gun to using the plaster to butter up the seams on the drywall. Why it was called that he had no idea, but she seemed to be having a good time while paying attention to detail.

When it started to get close to dinner, he decided he and Jilly would go out too. She was all for it but didn't want pizza. He'd noticed that about all three of the sisters—pizza wasn't high on their list of foods. As they were seated in a steakhouse, she told him what had happened to turn them off the usual treat for teenagers.

"That's all we could find to eat most nights. Someone would leave a slice or two in a box. Dumpster diving got to be a way of life for us if we wanted to eat." She shivered at the thought. "I'll never forgive Josh for doing that to us. The three of us often went to bed hungry or sick on something we'd had to share. And living in a nasty car during last winter had me happy for a hot shower when I got here, as well as being able to have clean underwear. It's the little things like that a person can miss when homeless."

"I'm sorry you had to go through that." She told him it wasn't his fault, but she did appreciate him making them a home. "I'm so happy to have you in our home that I have to pinch myself daily to remind myself I'm living with three of the most beautiful women around."

In answer to that, Jilly threw a tomato at him from her salad. They enjoyed their dinner. He was glad that Jilly liked her steak medium rare rather than well done. She even asked for extra sour cream for her potato, as he'd done.

Ian thought he could be a very happy man with the way things were falling into place for them. He knew there was still the uncle to have to take care of, but he didn't really foresee that becoming a huge issue. While he didn't know for sure, he was very hopeful.

By the time they were home, Lucy and Cybill were pulling in the drive. They looked exhausted but had gotten all the things they needed. Even the aprons for the staff were ordered. It was coming along nicely, Lucy told him, and was nearly asleep before she went up to bed. Tomorrow he'd tell her that he was a dad. Tonight that news was just for him, he thought.

Chapter 6

Josh wasn't happy. First, they took his money, and now they'd locked him out of the house. He wasn't stupid enough to say it was his home. The police and the attorney his nieces had hired had made it perfectly clear he had screwed up royally with the will. Josh was happy that so far, no one had mentioned he'd kicked the girls out. Perhaps no one cared. He certainly didn't.

He walked up to the house and smiled at the man standing in front of the front door.

"May I help you?" Josh explained to him that he'd not been able to get himself any clean clothing or even his toothbrush when he'd left that morning. "From what I understand, you didn't allow them girls to do that either."

So they did know about him and the girls. The man told him to move on.

"But I need just a few things from the house — my wallet

for one thing. I'm going to have to find a place to stay tonight until this thing is resolved, and without identification, that's not going to happen. Be a nice guy, why don't you, and let me go in for five minutes."

"No. I'm not even going to allow you to look into the house. Not until I'm told differently." Josh asked him what harm it could do. "Plenty from where I'm standing. You're a horrible person, and I'd rather cut off my arm than let you have a single comfort those girls didn't have while you lived it up in their family home."

Rolling his eyes at the man, Josh told him he'd give him two hundred dollars. He didn't even look interested, which he supposed was a good thing since he didn't have any cash on him. Josh wanted the credit cards to his brother's accounts so he could charge some clothing, as well as get the much needed room. No one used cash anymore anyway.

He sat down on the front steps and pulled out his phone. Someplace on it had to be the phone number for Lucy—the phone was his brother's. Apparently, when they'd gone on trips, they didn't take their phones so no one would bother them. He thought that was just as bad as him tossing the girls to the side of the road. How the hell were they to get in touch with him if he didn't have a phone? Whatever. Josh had always thought his brother and his wife were weird.

Finding the number proved to be telling for him as well. It didn't have just Lucy's name there. It actually only said, "Daughter #1." Shaking his head, he called the number. He waited for an entire minute before he realized the phone wasn't working. Checking the battery and seeing it was fully charged, he knew that at some point in her teaching him a lesson, Lucy had turned the phone off. He turned to the man still at the door.

"I don't suppose you could let me go in and use the phone, could you? Or yours. I don't care. I need to get in touch with my niece." The man didn't even look in his direction. "Are all people like you dicks, or is it just you? I swear to Christ, all I want to do is get my wallet so I can get a place to stay tonight. Perhaps get me a nice steak dinner. Hell, I'll even buy you dinner if you will just allow me inside."

"The credit cards have been canceled too." He looked at the woman in front of him and realized it was Lucy. "You aren't going to get into the house. We've decided, as a family, that we're going to sell it when we've gotten the things out of it that we want."

"I'm family. Why don't you just let me live in it until you have it sold? It's the least you can do for me." She just laughed and sat down on the chair she'd brought with her. "You're not a nice person, Lucy. What would your parents say about how you're treating me?"

"Great job? Kick him again while he's down? I don't know what they'd say about you dropping us off at the mall either, but I'm sure it wouldn't be very nice. I don't want you around, Josh. I don't even want to be around you. I've come here today to tell you that first of all, we're pressing charges against you. That in the very near future, you're going to prison. You should have been a great deal nicer to us, and you might have been able to live a long and free life away from prison." He told her they were all still alive. "Yes, we are, no thanks to you. We're happy too. I'm married to a wonderful man. We've adopted my sisters so they can be safe too."

"What if I were to kidnap you right now? Do you think he'd pay me to get you back? With all your sickly sweet happiness, do you think he'd care whether or not you were still alive?" She looked to his left, and he turned too. "Mother fuck, Lucy. What the fuck is that?"

"I believe it's a great black bear. If you were to look closer, you'd see there are six of them around you. As much as I hate to warn you, Josh, you even reach out to touch me, and you'll never be found. I do think, however, that would make it more difficult to sell the house." He asked her why, keeping his eyes on the bears he could now see. "The blood. Bears are messy killers. Did you know that? I mean, just look at their claws. Ian, please show him your massive claws, honey."

The big bear came closer to him, and it was all Josh could do to hold onto his bladder. When the thing put out his paw, not only did the monster stretch out his nails, but his paw alone looked as if it was bigger than Josh's entire head. He looked at Lucy when she thanked the bear, and he moved back.

"You're friends with bears now? Christ, what is this world coming to?" She said she was married to Ian. "Married to him? You've sullied yourself by marrying a shifter? What the fuck is wrong with you? Do you know what your parents would say?"

"Why do you keep bringing them up? You think they care about what happens to us? I don't know why I have to tell you this, but Josh, they're both dead and have been for some time. Why would I even care what my dead parents think about anything I do?" She looked around again, then back at him when a man dressed in jeans and a T-shirt joined her. "You've met my husband before, Josh. But today, he has a few things he'd like to say to you."

"Touch her or her sisters, and not only will you die, but I will personally make you suffer in ways that you cannot imagine. Understand me?" Josh nodded. He wasn't afraid of the big man. But when something made a noise next to him, he turned and looked right into the face of the biggest fucking bear he'd ever in his life seen. His bladder just simply let go. "This is my brother. He wants me to warn you that if I don't do exactly what I told you, if you touch my family, then he will. And he's a great deal meaner than any of the rest of us."

Josh could feel the bear's breath as it blew over his face. It was hot and incredibly sweet-smelling. It didn't take away from the fact that he would and could bite him. The teeth of the bear looked like ivory sharp knives in a mouth full of them. Even the bear's eyes, browner than he'd noticed before, looked mean. Intelligent, too, like he knew exactly what he was thinking.

"Lucian said to tell you he does indeed know what you're thinking. That he is reading your puny mind. Also, he said to tell you that you smell of piss. However, even before you wet yourself, he had your scent. That way, no matter where you are, where you would think to hide, he'd be able to find you quickly." Josh asked him what he'd done to warrant such hostility. "Breathing? Your heart beating? But on top of that, you not only nearly killed my sisters-in-law and wife by throwing them out of their home, but you were also paid for it. If I had my way, I'd tell my brother to end your fucking life right now."

"I have to tell you both. I just don't understand where this is all coming from." He had to think fast when the big bear touched his nose to his cheek. "Can you please tell your brother to get the fuck out of my face? I'm having a hard time thinking."

"You'd probably be better off if you didn't tax yourself with thinking. As for where this is coming from, you've been told, several times, why you're in deep shit with us. If you need it repeated to you yet again, I think it would be best if we gave you a little remembrance, so you don't have to be told again. You might just call it a lesson in remembering. What do you think?" Ian laughed as he continued. "It will be painful and ugly when the wound is scarred, but I think you'd remember it every time you looked at yourself in the mirror."

"No, no lessons." He finally stood up, but it didn't keep the bear from being right on his heels. "Lucy, why don't we just start over? You know, go back to the way it was, where I live in the house with the money put back into my account. You and your sisters can live with Ian here. It sounds like he's a fairly smart man, so I don't think you'd be without your own funds soon enough."

"He's worth more than my parents were. But it doesn't matter if he was broke or rich, you're not going to be living in the house, nor will I foot the bill for you living. You did notice that I said *living*. Because at the rate you're going, I don't see you doing that for very much longer. You're going to have to get it into your head sooner or later that you're not welcome in our lives. You've burnt that bridge. I'm not going to allow you anything. Not the house, money, or anything else you think you should have."

"This isn't fair at all. You're being incredibly selfish with this." He took a step closer to her, thinking if he could simply reach out —

Josh had no idea how it happened, but suddenly he was on his back with the large bear atop him. Not only that, but his great teeth were at his throat. If he'd had any kind of bowel movement in him, he surely would have shit himself. As it was, he pissed himself again.

"Please don't let him kill me." Ian laughed, and so did Lucy. "This isn't funny, you fucking idiots. Do you have any idea how close he is to just chomping my neck out? Pretty damned close."

"If he'd have wanted to, Josh, he could have taken your head off. But for now, he wants me to tell you that touching his family will get you killed." Josh told Ian he wasn't touching anyone. "No. Not when he took you down. But I did warn you that he could understand what you're thinking."

This was getting way out of hand. Nothing was going his way either. When the bear moved off him, Josh didn't move. The fucker could move fast, and he didn't want to have to be held down like that again.

A sudden move from the bear had him screaming in pain. Holding his face, hot blood seeping through his fingers, Josh knew he'd been cut. He didn't even want to think about what it was that cut him. Looking at his niece, he asked her what the hell had happened.

"I'd say you've been marked." She stood up, and Ian picked up her chair. A quick kiss between the two of them had his belly churn up. Or it could have been from the pain. Lucy finally knelt down to his level, and he wanted to spit in her eye. A growl from all the bears had him swallowing hard. "I'd get to the hospital if I were you, Josh. It looks to me like you've pissed someone off."

"You're going to pay for this, Lucy. I'm going to have the bills sent directly to you and that fucking husband of yours." She laughed as she stood up. "You mother fucking bitch. You're going to regret all of this. As soon as I'm up on my feet again, see if you don't. I'm done being fucking nice to you."

She was still laughing when she got into the car with Ian. Josh really was going to get her, and when he did, her living on the streets was going to seem like a sunny vacation. The bear growled at him again.

"You're all brave and shit being a bear, aren't you?" The bear, he would swear for the rest of his life, smiled at him. "When I get to the hospital, I'm going to tell everyone the McCrays are a bunch of savage bears. That'll have them hunting you down and killing the lot of you. You'll see."

The bear stood there for several seconds before it turned away from him. Josh started to stand up and was on his knees when the mother fucker pissed on him. Not just his head, but right in the wound that was still bleeding. Burning to the point that he was sick with the pain, Josh fell forward. Bumping his face on the filthy ground, the pain was too much, and he fainted dead away. Thankfully.

~*~

Lucy laughed every time she thought of Josh after they were home. She'd once thought he was an okay uncle, but now that she was older and he was in her space more, she realized what a fucking nasty piece of shit he was. Looking over at Ian when he busted out laughing, she asked him what was going on. Sitting on the couch with him, she was glad he wrapped his arm around her.

"He pissed on him." It took him three tries to tell her who had done it this time. "Lucian said he pissed him off again, and when he was getting ready to leave Josh, Lucian pissed all over his face and hands."

"Did someone take pictures?" There was a camera on the front stoop of the house, but she had no idea if it was working or not. "He really thinks things should go back to the way he wants them. Like we would just say okay, no hard feelings for leaving us to die."

"He's going to owe more than he can cover with his ass." Lucy told Ian she hoped he ended up in jail. "Or a loony bin. Lucian called an ambulance for him. He was unconscious while they were still there. If Josh mentions that a bear pissed on him or even cut him, they'll have him locked up so quickly it'll be months before he's out again."

"I thought most of the town knows you're bears." He nodded and told her why they'd still lock him up. "Oh. Okay, I guess letting it get out to everyone would be a bad thing. So just the town here knows for the most part. When he starts spouting off his mouth, then everyone pretends he's nuts.

I think he is anyway. I just can't believe how dense he was being with all this going on."

"I'm not sure if he's pretending to be that dense or he really is. Perhaps he thinks if he ignores the obvious long enough, whoever he's talking to will just let him get by with it. It might have worked for him before." Lucy didn't know. She'd not seen a great deal of her uncle growing up. "I'm sure there is a good reason for that as well. But I guess we'll never know. I'm going to see about getting us something to tide us over until dinner. What would you like to drink?"

"I love you, Ian." When he stopped moving, she stared at him. "I have been wanting to say that to you for a couple of days now, but it never seemed to be the right time. But I do. I think I have since I met you. Is this still the wrong time?"

"No. It's never the wrong time to tell someone you love them. I love you, as well. May I ask you how you figured it out?" She told him he was in her mind and heart all the time. "That's a wonderful answer, Lucy. You're the same with me."

He moved back into the room and sat on the couch again. However, this time he was further away from her than before. Lucy wanted to ask him what was going through his head right now but was almost afraid to. He might, for some reason, tell her she wasn't his type or something.

"I don't know what is going through your head right now, but you should know it's not nearly as bad as your face is telling me it is. I love you very much. Just think on that, all right?" She nodded. "Do I want to know what you were thinking?"

"More than likely not. I was afraid you were going to tell

me something like it's too late, or that you've changed your mind about us." He said he would never say that. "I guess I knew that, but my head and my heart rarely agree on things. Like this. What this is between us."

"What do you think this is between us?" She told him her thoughts. "Yes, we did marry quickly because of your uncle and his ability to perhaps take your sisters from you. While that was what rushed us, I would have married you at any time, uncle or not. This just made it so you were all safe. And mine."

"I'm afraid." He asked her of what. "Everything, I guess you could say. I'm afraid of something happening to the girls. Not so much now, but I do worry about them. That you'll really think this was a bad idea."

"Tell me what you think would be a reason for me to think this was a bad idea. I love you, Lucy. I have since the first time I saw you. I've never wanted anyone to be in my life as much as I do you. You're my reason for getting up in the morning, and for wanting to be a better man. I will admit I'm taking a lot of cold showers, but I can do that until you tell me you're ready for us to take the next step in our relationship." She asked him if that meant sex. "It means us making love. Sex is for relief, I think. Making love with you is what we'd be doing. A great deal of it, too, if you don't kill me the first time."

She laughed. It was a good time to laugh, and she felt better for it. "I do love you. I really do."

He pulled her to him and kissed her. As awkward as it was, it was that much and more soft and romantic. Ian could touch her, even wrap his arms around her, and she knew he loved her. When he picked her up from the couch and put her on his lap, she squeaked in delight.

"You are much too far away from me. I like it when you're so close, and I can smell you." He sniffed at her neck, just under her ears, and she felt a warm shiver go through her body. "I can smell how aroused you are too. Such a sweet, aromatic smell."

"The kids are in the house." He told her they'd gone out about an hour ago. They were at Demi's home. "How do you know they didn't get kidnapped along the way? Josh might— Oh yes, that feels wonderful. Why are they there?"

"Demi is filling out the paperwork for them to go to school this fall. Also, she's making sure the work permit is filled out for Jilly to work. I think Cybill is there because Mom is baking something for dinner." He looked at her, his brow cocked up on one side of his face. "I think we covered that the kids are out of the house, my dear. Is there anything I can do to assure you we're going to be all right if you start screaming your head off when you come?"

"Nope. I think you've covered it very well." Lucy giggled. "We're starting this married life out all ass backwards, don't you think? You're a father of two teenagers, with a wife who is afraid of her own shadow that you've never seen naked. Pretty screwed up if you ask me."

"I'm not asking you." He stood up with her in his arms, making her squeak again. "Now. I'm going to set you down on your feet. You run up the stairs while I lock up the house. Go."

Taking off for the stairs, she was at the top of them when she heard the lock engage on the front door. Ian told her to go once again, and she rushed to the bedroom. While she didn't have anything sexy to wear to bed on their sort of wedding night, Lucy figured he'd not care if she was naked. So that was what she did. Stripping down to her warm skin, she stood there by the bed, waiting for him to come up the stairs to join her.

Unsure of how to stand without looking foolish, Lucy changed her stance three times before she thought she'd just wing it. When the door opened up, she stood there, holding her breath until she saw him.

"You're beautiful." Her face heated up to the point where she had to put her cooler hands on her cheeks. "I wasn't sure what to expect when I sent you up here. Something like you'd be hiding in the bathroom. Or in the closet. But this? This is perfect. You're perfect."

"I feel silly." He asked her why. "You're completely dressed, and I'm not. I have no idea what I thought you'd be doing when you got here, but not that...you know what? Thank you. I'm so happy you find me beautiful."

He moved into the room — glided was a better word for it. He took his shirt up and over his head, and she could see his chest was covered in dark hair. Fur, she supposed it should be called. Each step Ian took toward her, he'd take something else off. A shoe, then his other one. His belt went the way of his shirt. Even as he stood in front of her with only his boxers on, she thought him the most beautiful creature she'd ever seen.

"May I touch you?" He growled, and her pussy pulsated with heat. "You keep that up, my beautiful bruin, and I'll come without you even touching me."

"Bruin is brown." She looked at his face and noticed he was having a hard time speaking. "Bruin is the word for a brown bear. I'm a black bear. I have no idea why I'm telling you that. It's all I can do just to stand here and breathe. Touch me wherever you want. If you come before me, then I'll make you come again and again."

Lucy touched her fingers to his shoulders. They were tight with muscles. Running her fingers down the large vein along the outside of his arm, she loved how his breathing changed. How he was no longer just breathing in and out, but panting. As soon as she touched her fingers to his nipple, which was as hard as hers were, she leaned into him and licked the tiny morsel, then bit down.

"Holy Christ."

She didn't stop or slow after he held onto the wall behind her. His arms up and over her head gave her just enough room to do as she pleased, which was to please him as much as she possibly could before he snapped.

Touching him in different places brought sounds from him that she was sure were only for her to hear. Touching his navel brought a moan when she licked the indentation. Nipping at his elbow made him cry out. Every place was a new sound, and every new sound made her so wet she was sure she was making Ian wilder for her.

"Enough." She found herself against the wall behind her. Giggling when he stripped off his boxers, she reached out to wrap her hand around him. "No. You touch me, and I'm going to come all over you. I need to fill you. I have to mark you as mine. If I come right now, I'm not even sure I'll remain upright, much less conscious. My turn to make you suffer, my heart. And suffer in the greatest way I know how."

Chapter 7

Ian felt his bear run along his skin. Lifting Lucy up, so her mouth was in front of his, he kissed her as savagely as he felt. His inner beast was tearing at his soul to claim their mate. As soon as her feet touched the floor, he lifted her up against his body, and she wrapped her legs around him. Ian entered her hard and quick. While she was not a virgin, he knew he'd still hurt her.

"I'm so sorry." Even as he said the words, he knew whatever was going on between him and his beast was far from over. Pulling back, trying to disengage himself from the beast, Ian felt the snarl of his anger as he told Lucy once again how very sorry he was.

"Please stop, Ian, it hurts so badly."

Instead of slowing his beast took her harder, Ian's body no longer his own. Nor could he hear her after a minute. All he could hear inside of his head was the roar of the bear.

The triumphant sound of claiming his mate. Then his hands morphed into his other half.

Ian was no longer in control. No longer making love to his wife, but hurting her through the monster that was taking him. But still, he came. His body releasing into hers was more painful than he'd ever experienced. Ian wanted to stop, wanted to tend to his bride. He realized then that it wasn't over just yet.

When she screamed, he looked down at her body and could see the claws of him ripe with her blood as they pierced her flesh. Wounds that were created when the claws from his bear slid through her body and touched his belly.

Blood slid down her body and onto the floor. He begged his bear to release her, telling him that he was killing their mate. All he did in reply was to dig deeper until Ian was sure she had been killed by him. Then she was lifted from his body to be held up by only the claws of his bear.

Laying her on the bed, Ian felt sick. When his bear left him, literally left his body to be on his own, Ian could only watch as he licked the wounds he'd made clean. Why he was bothering, Ian didn't know. With her being only human, there wasn't any way she could have survived this. And he knew he wouldn't either. He knew as surely as he watched her, he'd join her in death.

Help me, young McCray. Shaking his head, he told his bear to leave him be. To let his mate be at peace. *If you do not help me, I will have to wait another generation. I wish this to end now, young McCray. Help me save our mate.*

Getting up, blinded by his tears, he rolled Lucy to her

stomach so his bear could clean and close the wounds there. When there was little else they could do for her body, Bear lifted his mate up and held her as Ian stripped the sheets off the bed. The mattress was, he knew, ruined.

Once she was lying on clean linen, Ian took her hand into his. It was cold, deathly cold, and her pale skin was turning blue as he held her. Looking at Bear, not sure what else to call him, he asked him what he'd done.

I have saved us. Shaking his head, Ian told him he'd killed the only thing in the world that he'd ever love. *Nay, young McCray. I have finally finished something that was started with the first McCray. The very first bear-to-man shifter. You and this young maid were born to be the ones who will carry on and keep the history alive.*

"She's dead. You've killed her." Bear took his other hand and laid it upon Lucy's chest. It was the barest of beats, but her heart was beating quickly and ever so quietly. "I don't understand. What did you do to her? She'll hate me if she lives."

She will live. As will you, my son. I have been awaiting a bride that would be strong enough to take the magic I have given her. Waiting, too, for you to be born to keep her safe. All is right in the world, Ian James McCray. You will see once she is awake. Ian asked what he'd done. *It would be better to start at the beginning, don't you think? To tell the story in a way that you will understand the urgency of what has happened here today. The reason there were times when you felt I was not a part of you. That you and I had separate paths in mind.*

"You're not a part of me now." Bear nodded. He told him

it was the way it had to be to save her. "You had to kill her to save her? That can't be right. You know that, don't you?"

I know she is bear, the same as you. Your children will be born as bears, full-blooded, that will breed bear cubs for as long as the world turns. It had to be done, or I would have had to wait another millennium, decades and decades of waiting to see if this mate would survive, unlike the others. You know what I say is true. You have uncles, back along your lines, that bore no children. Had no mate. It was because, sadly, their mates could not survive. They weren't able to take the magic this one now holds. He asked him what sort of magic. "*Ah, that is the most important question you could ask of me. The magic of all the bears. Magic that will save races of beings because of your and your mate's flowing through them. There will be many born, Ian James, many offspring of the two of you, that will be stronger for it. They'll be able to blend into towns. Become working men and women. But their bears will be forever stronger.*

"Why? I mean, we're a strong family now. We have never been ill or in trouble. We've been around for so long I can count back the generations for many years. Why do you think nearly killing Lucy would make us stronger?" The bear asked him if he could tell him the story now. "Yes. I need to know why we've made her suffer. Because you know as well as I do that she suffered greatly, that she might not ever forgive me for what I did to her today."

She will not only forgive you, Ian James, but she will have knowledge to pass on from this transformation that even you won't know. Bear sat on the floor, his body taking the shape of a man, much older than Ian thought his parents were. "I am the first of the shifters from bear to man. All the McCray lines are of my blood. They think — which is a good thing, I suppose — that they were born men that could shift to bear. But the opposite is true. We are and always will be the very first shifter bears. It was deemed so when the lady of the lands, the mother of earth, found me suffering a wound that was seeping the life from my body. She freed me then, healing my wound while she was there. Then she sat me down to speak to me. As a man, not a bear."

"You said you were the first. Are you telling me you've been waiting for me to be born since there were bears on this earth?" Bear told him almost. "Then, you had parents. They were bears. How did you become McCray? I'm sorry. So many questions are racing in my mind that I feel overwhelmed by it."

"As you should be. Yes, I had parents. They were bears too. A black bear and a brown one. I was born black. My siblings were born shades of brown. It mattered little what the color of our fur was. We were family." He hummed a tune then, and Ian smiled. "There it is that wonderful smile of yours. Once I was freed, she changed me to man, so anyone coming upon us would think it a woman speaking to a man. There were few that wandered the earth then, but it was safer for us both. I told her, once I was healed by her touch that I would gladly do whatever she needed of me. Go wherever she needed me to go. I was her servant for my life."

"I guess she took you up on your offer." They both laughed, and he realized how warm Lucy's hand was now, How her heartbeat was stronger, and he could hear it better. Kissing her wrist where her pulse beat best, he looked into her face and saw that she was awake. "I love you, Lucy. I'm so sorry."

"You did nothing wrong, Ian. Not a thing." She looked at the bear/man as he sat there by her bedside. "I'm to tell you from your own mate that you had better be bringing her home a treat when you leave this earth. She will not tolerate you coming home empty handed."

Bear laughed, tears streaming down his weathered face. Kissing her other hand, he told Lucy he had just the gift for his lady. That he, too, was looking forward to leaving this earth. Ian asked him why he was to leave.

"I was only to wait for the strongest female to come to this family. You have found each other. And in that, my time here is finished. You will, the two of you, take over the duties I was asked to do for the mother of earth." Ian asked if they were to wait on the next strongest female. "Nay, that was for me to do. What you are to do is to fill the earth with magic. Spread it from one end of this earth to the other. The world will honestly be a better, happier place now that the two of you have been found. In saying that, a man, an attorney of sorts, will come to see you. Paperwork, you understand. So that the two of you can get paid."

"All right. But I don't understand. I don't have any magic. You said that Lucy does, but I'm just a shifter bear. Nothing more." Bear told him he was always so much more than a bear. Even before he gave them the magic. "What sort of magic are you talking about? To me, I don't feel any different than before."

"You are. We both are." Lucy stood up and stretched.

Her skin was alive with something, it seemed. It was then he realized it was her bear. It moved along her skin in not just black fur, but all the colors a bear of their kind could be. "The magic we have will now help species we are losing by disease and manmade things. Help the ones that are already here and keep the future species healthy. Not just bears, but all animals. With our magic, we can help with not just the livelihood of bears, but the life of the earth for having more of them. More bears mean there will be more plants grown because of their droppings. Other species of animals will survive because they can prey on them to survive. This would include man too. We're to help with groves of plants for the different breeds of our kind. Our magic is vast, Ian. It's there for us to use for every animal and human."

Ian was beginning to understand. Not only that, but information, long thick volumes of it, seemed to be filling his mind. Needs were listed for them to take care of. What they could do for the future as well as the animals that were now suffering. Lucy was doing that. He didn't know why he knew it was from her, but he knew it to be true.

Laying his head back on the wall, he felt it filling him. Information he would never have known about animals long dead. The reason some of the animals they were to care for were suffering—the immediate and the future things, the magic they could use to help with these projects. The need to get started on them energized him, making him want to get started as soon as he could arrange it.

"I must go." Ian shook his head, asking him why he'd leave him without a bear. "Nay, I have only shared the space in you with your own bear. He has been dormant these past years, learning all I could teach him with the hope that someday the two of us would no longer have to share you. You can feel him, Ian James. I'm sure you can."

He could. The bear was there as before, but different. Stronger too. Standing up when Lucy did, he felt the weight of his duty hit him hard. What if he couldn't do what was needed of him? The pop to the back of his head was a reminder that he had a partner in this, and she wasn't someone to mess with. They would do whatever was needed. Of that, he knew he didn't have to doubt.

Pulling Lucy to him, he kissed her on the mouth, then held her close to him as they said their goodbyes. Bear shifted to a bear again just as two male bears and a female joined him in the room.

"My mate and wife, Honey." Lucy hugged her, then he did as well. "Your uncles, Ian. James McCray, the first male who lost his mate to the magic. And this is Ian McCray, another uncle that lost his mate. They have come to thank you, both of you, for being the ones to carry on. They told me several decades ago that it would be you. Even before you were born, they told me it would be Ian James who bore the magic. It only took a small hint to your mother to have her name you as such. I hope you know how much was riding on your being born and having a strong mate. As it is, it will be difficult to live out eternity with these two since they were right."

"Thank you for having such confidence in me." They told him it was his mate that they knew would bring it to the earth. "Yes, well, had I known, I would have told you that with Lucy, there is nothing she couldn't do."

The four bears hugged them again, then one by one, they faded out. The last to leave them was Honey. Lucy asked her what her mate's name had been. At her laughter, Ian knew that it was going to be epic.

"He is Holland McCray. We called him Hollie." Honey looked at him. "You're a good man, Ian James. I know you'll be good at this task set before you." She looked at Lucy. "The child you carry now, my dear, will be the first in the family to be born with all the magic you now have. Also, please tread carefully around Joshua Jackson. He will try and harm those that you love."

She faded away soon after speaking. It occurred to him what she'd said to Lucy about a child, but it seemed to take Lucy a few seconds longer. When she screamed and hugged him, Ian thought he could take on the world and win. He was going to work hard so as not to fail any of the ones he was set to help. And especially not his own family.

~*~

Josh woke, startling himself as to where he was and how he'd gotten there. As soon as he opened his mouth to yell for help, everything came rushing back to him. Lying back on the bed, he was careful as he touched his face to see how badly he was damaged. Of course, all he figured out was that his face was completely covered. Even one of his eyes was covered in some kind of soft material. Finding the little button he knew would get him some help, the person on the other end of the thing asked him if he needed anything.

"I need to see how badly the bear tore at me." The person

asked him what he meant. "A bear. Damn it. A bear cut me up when I was trying to get into my house. And it's my fucking house too."

"Sir, you're going to have to watch your language while you're on the intercom." He did not argue with her. He supposed there might be some little kiddies around. "I'll have one of the nurses come in and help you with your request. However, if you would bring your tray table to you, you'll find a mirror on the drawer. Can you reach it?"

"Yeah, I got it." He had to reach out a little more than he should have but didn't fall. Lucky for him. Josh almost told her his table was broken when it suddenly popped open, and he saw the mirror. "Stupid thing. Smallest damned mirror I ever seen."

As soon as he got it adjusted, he wished with all he was worth he'd not bothered. The way his face was swollen, he was sure he shouldn't have been able to speak. Looking up at the nurse who came into the room, he watched her close the little drawer that hid the mirror from his view.

"It looks much worse than it really is." Nodding, he asked her what the bear had done. "Bear? I don't know, Mr. Jackson. We were only told that you were in a freak accident that cut into your face."

"A bear did this." The nurse didn't comment when he repeated what had done this to him. She checked his IV as well as the fluid-filled bags that were hung just behind him. "What is it I'm looking at here? Am I going to be disfigured? Is there a doctor I can talk to about having it fixed so I can look at myself once in a while?"

"You've had your cheek split open, but it's been sewn together. The surgeon said as the swelling goes down, he'll go in and tighten the stitches up, which will help lessen the scarring." He told her he didn't want any scars. "I don't know anything about your wounds, Mr. Jackson. I do know we're to make sure you're not in any pain, and that we change the dressings. I can, if you want, show you the way you've been taken care of when we take the bandages off in the morning."

"Yes. That's what I want. I need to know how badly I'm going to sue that fucking McCray." She asked him if he meant the local family of McCrays. "Yeah, you know them? Sorriest bunch of people I ever met. One of them married my niece and took my home away from me. Do you believe that shit? Just waited for me to go out to get me some groceries or something, and they had the locks changed on it and even raided my bank account."

"Without the donations from the McCrays, you'd still be waiting in the emergency department while we transferred you to a larger hospital. Now, if you don't need anything else, Mr. Jackson, I have more grateful patients to care for."

"What the hell did I do to you? Shit in your oats or something? I'm just telling you that those fucking shits have done this to me. They're bears. All of them. Did you know that?" Not another word from her as she stood there. "Listen. I'm guessing we can agree to disagree. Right now, I need something for my hurting. Can you bring me something for it? I'm hurting pretty badly right now—I'm guessing it's because I've been talking so much. Also, you remember to charge this to them too."

When she left him, Josh had a feeling he not only wouldn't get anything for his pain, he'd bet anything she was going to make sure he didn't have any services that were required of her. Like fluffing his pillows when he needed it. Changing out his sheets. Even the sponge bath might be better left undone. She'd more than likely scald him.

Why the hell couldn't people see others the way they really were? The McCrays had money, he supposed. They were generous with it too. Because he'd badmouthed them, he was going to be shit on the entire time he was in here.

Josh dozed off and on for the rest of the evening. He did get his medications. However, he was sure they'd waited for him to be sleeping before they brought them to him. Waking to have his blood pressure taken was another dig to him badmouthing the McCrays. As soon as he would settle down, someone would turn on the light in his room and ask him a million questions before he could get his head awake enough to answer them.

Deciding to take notes on the way he was being treated, he realized the mistake in that too. If he asked them for paper and a pen, he'd have to explain what he was doing. That, he was sure, wouldn't go over too well. Even his dinner wasn't anything he'd eat if he had his way.

"Why am I not getting a good meal? You're doing this, aren't you?" She asked him what he meant. "Since I told you what the McCrays were doing to me, you've been treating me like I'm a big pile of dump. I'll tell you right now, I don't care for it."

"Mr. Jackson, I'm not sure if you're aware of this or not,

but you're not the only post-op person on this floor. Since you were brought here, we've had sixteen other patients brought to us, three of which were critical." She looked at his meal, then at him. "If you think you can eat a full dinner without tearing out any of the stitches, then I'll order you one. However, the doctor, silly him, thought you should be on a liquid diet so as not to have to go back into surgery to repair any damage you might bring to yourself. Your cheek was open to your jaw, sir. I asked in the event you asked me again. Doctor Martin said he could count your teeth from the wound in your face. Also, your eye socket was damaged, which is the reason your eye is covered, so you don't strain it trying to focus. But, if you're smarter than the surgeon who put you back together, then, by all means, let me order you a three-course meal."

"Nobody told me all that." She asked him if he'd asked anyone for information other than this morning. "No. What about waking me to get medications or my blood pressure? You're doing that to be mean too, aren't you?"

"When you're on my floor after surgery, we take your blood pressure every hour for the first six hours. If there is no change and you seem to be all right, then we downgrade it to every two or four." She looked at his chart. "Medication is given to you every six hours, so you're not suffering and tensing up to cause damage to the stitches in your face. Keeping ahead of the pain is the only way to keep you from having to have too much of it at one time. Again, if you're smarter than the people that do this for a living, I can arrange it, so you have your pain medications when you ask for them. It's the least I can do for you, being that you seem to think you're my only patient today."

When she finally left him after making him feel like shit, he laid there on the bed and wondered if he could get her fired. There wasn't any reason for her to be treating him like this. He was a paying customer, just like if he'd been eating in a fancy restaurant. Well, he wasn't paying, but someone would. Lucy and those sisters of hers were getting themselves into deeper shit every day.

The television was on a station he didn't care for. Before asking how to change the channels, he worked on it himself. There was no telling what she'd do to him if he asked for a little help with the stations.

"May I help you, Mr. Jackson?" He told her he was changing the channels. "You've pressed the nurse's button. The channel button is at the top."

Three more times he accidentally called the nurse's station and managed to turn the television on and off four times before he just quit. He'd have to have one of them come in here, and it just wasn't worth the time to piss them off again. Josh wanted to stay on their good side in case he needed something important. He couldn't think what that would entail, but he held his tongue as things were moving around him for the night. Drinking his dinner wasn't all that fulfilling, but he didn't complain all that much. Even using the straw, he'd found in the tabletop thing had gotten him into Dutch with the nurses. How the hell was he to know that sucking on a straw to eat this shit was going to be bad for him? Finally, he asked for a list of things he wasn't supposed to do.

"We don't have a list like that." The person who came into his room just before his tray was taken away huffed at him several times before she looked all through his table and bedside table to make sure there were no more straws or other contraband, as she called it. "We expect people to use their noddle after having their face put back together. Did it hurt you when you used the straw? I imagine it did. Yet you kept right on using it, didn't you?"

"How the hell else was I supposed to get this stuff in my belly?" She said the thing would have been for him to ask before he used a straw. "I know that now. How the hell am I supposed to know all this when you don't tell me?"

"Was there a straw on your tray, Mr. Jackson? No, there wasn't. Do you want to know why there wasn't? Because you're not supposed to have one. If you were to look on the menu that came with your meal, you'd see in bold letters not to give you a straw."

"I thought you were just being mean to me again." She moved to the door, but he could tell she was ready to pop him a good one. "Look, lady. I'm in here because the McCray men are all bears. If you'd been there with me, you'd have pissed yourself, it was that scary. I think you could cut me some slack on not knowing how to keep my stitches in place after a bear attacked me."

"You keep talking like that, Mr. Jackson, and I'm going to have you transferred to the fourth floor. Where all the other people having those sorts of thoughts are currently staying." She laughed. It was a mean little laugh. "I might just send you there so we can have some peace for a while. You're the neediest patient I've dealt with."

"Thank you."

She left him before he could ask her for some graham crackers he'd seen being passed out earlier. Josh thought about calling her back on the nurse thing but decided they'd probably tell him they weren't for him. Yes, he thought, there were just too many rules he was expected to know and follow. After he was home again, he was going to write a book on staying in the hospital. It might well be a best seller. People would want to know what he was learning the hard way, and he'd be hailed as a genius. Josh laughed a little, then stopped.

His face was really beginning to pain him badly. Again, he'd suffer through it without making too much of a fuss. It was the least he could do today. Yeah, like that was going to happen. Picking up the call button again, he told them he was ready for his medications and left it at that. He was going to call them every five minutes if he had to. Waiting five minutes, by his estimation, was about all he could take, so he called them again.

Josh figured the only way to get good service was to make a stink. Yes sir, he was going to write a book about all this. Just as soon as he took care of Lucy and her sisters.

That was something he had to think on too. How to not just get back into his home, but to get his money back. Also, to stay clear of the McCrays. It was their fault, he figured. Who else would have helped his nieces get into his account and kick him from his home? He really loved that old house. His brother should have invited him to stay with them more, too, he thought. He was, after all, his blood brother. Those girls were secondary to him, he realized. He and Donald were related by the same parents. The girls were just his and his wife's.

Josh was going to bring that up the next time Lucy started talking about how he had no rights to the house and money. The will should have said what he'd written it out to be. Blood was thicker than water, he'd always heard. Not that he knew what that meant in this circumstance, but damn it, he wanted his home and money back.

That was going to be taken care of first. When he got out of here, he was going to demand that he was allowed back into the house. He had been injured by them. They should want him to live in the house. He'd bring that up too, by god. Josh was going to start laying down the law with his nieces.

Chapter 8

Ian didn't know what to do. It was as if every cell in his body was vibrating. Not just a little either. It was like they were all riding a bronco ride at the same time. He lifted his head slowly when his dad said his name.

"Boy, are you all right?" He said no. "I was just talking to your wife, and she said you've been chosen for some kind of big deal. Want to talk about it?"

"Dad, I'm in deep shit here. I can't make my mind stay still for even a second." Dad sat across from him. "Did Lucy tell you she's a bear?"

"She did. I don't know how that happened. She said you didn't change her. Not really. I haven't any idea what is supposed to have happened." Ian told him he wasn't entirely sure either. "Ian, you're sounding a little wigged out. Why don't you start from the beginning and we'll work it out? All right?"

"We had sex." It wasn't as hard to admit that to his dad as he'd thought it would be. Maybe if he'd not been so messed up. "My bear left me. I mean, he was sitting across from me while he told us what was going to be going on. He's old, dad. I mean, he was really old, and he went away with his wife and other family members."

"Were they having a picnic?" Ian growled at his dad. "Son, I'm trying my best to understand this. But you're just saying things like I should understand. What do you mean, his family was there? I was understanding that this bear was our family."

"Okay. Do you remember any uncles called James and Ian? They would have been from different generations." Dad told him he'd been named for them. "Yes, that's what they told me. That I was named for them, and they thought I was going to be the one that had his mate survive the change. All of the ones before me, their mates couldn't handle the magic. Understand?" Dad said he did.

The best he could, he explained to his dad what had happened. He had to jump around a little, forgetting a little detail or something like that. After he was finished telling his dad, he just sat there staring at him. Ian actually felt a little better after explaining it to him. It sort of cleared it up for him as well. The telling of it made it feel like it made sense.

"I'm not being smart-alecky or anything, son, but I do have a few questions. All right with you?" Ian told his dad he'd answer them as best he could. He, too, was having trouble getting it all straight. "This bear, he never told you his name? You just called him Bear?"

"I did. He didn't seem to mind it either. His wife, she told me his name was Holland, and they called him Hollie. But he never said that to us. Why?" Dad said he was getting to that. "Dad, I don't know all we're supposed to do or even how to make it work, but Lucy, she seems to have a better handle on this than I do."

Lucy entered the room with a large platter of food. Carrots and cheese with crackers. There were also some meats. He was too buzzed to talk. Even though he was feeling better, he didn't think he was ready for food yet. Lucy kissed him and then turned to his dad. She asked him what he wanted to know.

"Ian told me his name was Holland. They called him Hollie. Right?" Lucy told him that was right. His wife was Honey. "Yes, Honey. Do you know why she was called Honey? I think I do. They could get honey to sell without any issues. Jars and jars of it. Honeycombs too. That was how families at the start of this bloodline would have been able to trade for things they'd need in the house."

"That makes sense, I guess. I mean, being a bear, she'd be able to know not only where it was, but also how to get it." Dad told them that was correct. "Hollie told us he was the original shifter from bear to man. Not man to bear. I didn't know there was a difference. He said it was a huge deal for him to have been the first shifter."

"Yes. It's written down in the Bible your mom has that has been passed down from generation to generation since Holland was born." Ian asked his dad when Hollie had died. "Well, I don't know that. I've contacted your mom, and she's bringing the Bible here now. We might not get to the bottom of this, but we'll be able to make some headway in it. What sort of magic do you have? I mean, have you figured that out yet?"

Lucy stood up and changed her clothing several times. Just one outfit to the next. When she put out her hand, a tall glass of what appeared to be tea appeared. Dad asked Ian if he knew what they were supposed to do.

"Use magic to help other bears populate. I'm not sure what that is supposed to entail completely, but I have a feeling it's going to be along the lines of making sure they're healthy and have a place to live. Things like that." Dad asked him what else he might have to do. "To be honest with you, Dad, I think it's going to depend on what is needed at the time. Each person or group we help, we'll have whatever magic is needed to make sure we can help them. If they need shelter? We help them with that. Food? Again, we make sure that the grounds will yield enough for them to eat on. Also, we'll be able to help barren females and males be able to have a child. I have bits and pieces of things like that in my mind. That's why I believe it's going to be dependant on the situation."

Mom came into the house with the big Bible. She didn't seem all that happy about something, but she said she'd tell them later. When Dad asked her about Hollie McCray and when he'd died, she stared at him for several seconds before speaking.

"I looked when you asked me about him. There isn't a date on the year he died. It just says.... Well, let me show you. It's the strangest entry I've ever read." Lucy brought the Bible to him, and they looked for his name. "Also, those names you asked me about. Ian and James? Well, there isn't a name there for either of them. I don't know what that means either. I thought they were wed, and then they died. I nearly put the book away and was going to tell you I couldn't find it. Then I looked up Hollie. Go ahead, Lucy. You tell him what it says."

"Holland Phillip McCray. Born in fourteen twelve." Lucy looked at him. "Fourteen twelve? Do you know how long that man has been around? Christ love a duck."

She handed Ian the book, and he found the entry. "Hollie was born at home. His date of death says unknown. Then it has a notation here I can't read. Not that I can't read it. I just don't know what language it's in." Ian leaned back in his chair. "Whoever wrote this knew more about this than just an unknown date of death. Until you mentioned it, I had no idea there was a family Bible. Dad, this is scary."

"So, Hollie said you two were born for this, and that Lucy here was strong enough to live through the changing as well as the magic coming to you." Ian told his mom that was what he said. "And now that he's gone, you two will take over his job and be around until the next generation or whatever is born. Son, that could be an exceptionally long time."

"We'll be paid. I don't know how much or even if it's enough for us to live on, but someone somehow makes sure we can do what we need to do when we are needed. We're to meet some guy soon that will have us sign off on some of the paperwork we'll need to have in order to get paid. I don't know what we'd have to sign, before you ask. Hollie was somewhat vague about it. Also, you should know that it's not just Ian and I that will be around forever. All of the family will be as well, he told me." Dad told Lucy he didn't want to be around forever. "I don't think you have to be if you don't want to. But Alden, don't you want to be here for all your grandchildren? All of them? I know I'd like for you to be around for my kids and their kids too. Oh, I'm going to have a baby. Honey told me."

"I'm sorry. What?" Lucy smiled at Ian and then repeated that she was going to have a child to his mom. "You're going to have a baby? Lucy, that should have been the first words out of your mouth when I got here. Oh, my goodness. More grandchildren. I'm the luckiest grandma in the world. Of course, we want to be around. Alden, grandchildren bouncing on our knees for all time."

"But this could be hundreds of years. Hundreds and hundreds of years. Whatever will we do in all that time? Not to mention, if nobody dies, then there won't be anyone for our family to marry that won't be related to them." Ian laughed. "I don't think this is the least bit funny, son. This is some serious business."

"It is. But that's just about the funniest excuse I've heard for not wanting to live forever. I'm sorry, Dad. You have to admit that not having a mate to marry is funny." Dad just glared at him. "Dad, I'm still dealing with this the best I can. Lucy and I haven't had much more time than you have to get used to this. The magic? What she showed you is the tip of the iceberg on what we can do."

Ian put out his hand. This was what had him freaking out when his dad had arrived. Concentrating on just having the flame of fire in his palm, it appeared. After it was glowing hot, he changed it to a snowball. Then he split it in half so that one side was frozen ice, the other hot flames.

"I don't have any idea what I might use that for, but I can do it. Also, I can do this." He laid both his hands on the table and thought of a Thanksgiving feast. The food, all of his favorites of the meal, appeared. "It's real too. I've eaten some of it. And after I get all I want out of it, I can put it away."

"To feed bears/people. Okay. That would be helpful. A healthy person can have healthy children." He nodded at his dad. "I'm not saying this is bogus or anything. Don't take that from this. But why? Why not just give you enough money to help people? Why magic?"

Ian didn't know. He didn't know a lot of things. But it was there. The magic, the ability to help. But why? Why indeed was there magic? What could he do to help bears reproduce when there were medical treatments that would fix that without him? For that matter, how the hell was he supposed to fix that? Touch the bellies of females? Was he supposed to make sure they were having sex at the right time?

After his parents left, he was no closer to knowing anything than he'd been before. He wanted to be able to sit down with Hollie and ask him questions. What if Hollie was wrong about him having to find a replacement for when his time was finished? When he had to find the next person to take over for him, would he be killing young unsuspecting women too? That wouldn't be something he'd do. Ian wasn't sure even Lucy would want him to do that.

"I have about a million and ten thousand questions. How

about you?" Ian told her he was sure he could double it. "Yeah, just what I was thinking too. This is insane. I mean, who would have thought that an act of sex could bring out so much confusion as well as pain? Why us? Why did you fit the bill for whatever he has going on? I'm not saying you'd not be great at this job, but we have more questions than we should for this sort of thing. Don't you agree?"

"Even when I voice my concerns, even to myself, they open up about a thousand more concerns than before." He held Lucy to him as soon as she sat down beside him. "I wonder if there is a way we could just quit this and tell someone we're not doing it. I'll help people out, that I have no trouble with. But this is crazy nuts."

The knock at the door didn't faze either of them. When someone rang the doorbell, he saw Hinkley go to the door with Lucy right behind him. It was nice having someone around that would do things like this. Not having to talk to anyone unless they wanted to. Leaning back on the couch, he was shocked when a strange voice started talking.

The woman that entered the room with Hinkley was glowing. He didn't have any idea what she might be, but whatever it was, he had the feeling she could simply kill them without a bat of her eyes. The fact that she was smiling at him didn't lessen his fear of her.

"My goodness, he surely did pick a beautiful couple, didn't he?" Lucy asked the woman who she was. "Oh, my. My manners. I'm the mother of all creatures, Gaea. And as such, I've been around a very long time and have had dealings with Hollie and his job. I've come to talk to the two of you about what he might have convinced you has happened. You've nothing to worry about if you've not signed anything. You've not, have you?"

"No. The man was supposed to come around soon, but we've not seen him." She smiled at him. "Why do I have the feeling the confusion we're experiencing now is nothing compared to what you're about to tell us?"

Her laughter chimed around the room. It was that too, the sound of a well-balanced wind chime. When she sat down on the couch across from him, Lucy joined him on the other couch again. The woman asked Hinkley to bring in something very sweet. That they were all going to need it before too much longer.

~*~

Gaea watched the two of them as they sat before her. They were a beautiful couple, but she knew Hollie picking them had nothing to do with that. Instead, he would pick people that would have been stupid, or so he thought with these two. They were smarter than even she had given them credit for being.

"You said he was going to *convince* us of a job. I'm assuming all this bullshit he told us is just that. Bullshit." Gaea laughed and told Ian it was the way he did things. "What is his deal? I mean, has he done this sort of thing before? If so, I'm going to murder his ass."

"You cannot. Though there are a lot of people that wish he was dead. He's nothing but a trickster, one that prays on people he believes to be too dumb to realize what they've gotten into. In this, Hollie is trying his best to have you take over, not his job, which is what I'm assuming he told you, but his prison sentence. He's been in a magical jail for a long time." Lucy asked her how he'd gotten out. "He has from time to time. Not lately. I thought the chains on his person were enough to hold him. I know now that not only was he able to escape, but someone gave him enough magic that he could come here with the two of you. Did he harm either of you?"

Ian explained how he'd nearly killed his mate. When she asked Lucy to stand, she could see that this, too, was magic. Running her hand over the places Ian told her he'd seen the claws come through, she could feel the magic that had been put upon the young woman to make them believe she was being injured.

"He said I was with child. That's not true either, is it?" Gaea said she was sorry. "It's fine. To be honest with you, I didn't want to conceive a child by Ian in that way. It was too violent and painful."

"Again, I'm so very sorry. If you'd not mind, I can explain things to you about his visit and why he's done this." Ian and Lucy both said they would love to hear it. "Good. His name is Holland, as he told you. Also, he was, at one time, a bear. However, he's not related to you at all. The names he used would have made you think so, but sadly, they're nothing more than just things he's picked up from others in your family. Mind reading."

"So what does he want? You said he was serving time." Gaea told them that Lucy was an immortal and would be for as long as the world had magic. Gaea had been the one to give it to her. "I don't know in human years what that might be, but I'm assuming a very long time."

"It is. Hollie is, as I said, a trickster. It's a label that was put upon him when he gained magic for a deed he was to have done. However, it wasn't until later it was discovered he had caused the trouble rather than being the one that had stopped it. Long story short, Hollie was more trouble than the average magical creature." Lucy asked if he'd harmed anyone. "Killed them, yes, several hundred people, as a matter of fact. He was responsible for sinking a boat with hundreds of people on it. He put an iceberg in their way, and it was a disaster even before so many were saved. Hollie did help with the rescue by turning boats toward those in need. But the damage had been done, and a great deal of magic had been his before it was discovered. His magic, because we all thought him to be a hero, was given to him as gifts. It wasn't until later we figured out he'd been the one to cause the incident in the first place."

"Why didn't someone take it back? I mean, that would seem to be the most logical thing to have done." She told Ian that once you have magic, it's not that easy to take it back. Sometimes impossible. "I'd figure out a way. Even if I had to remove his head. He hurt my mate. Not just a little, either."

"Lucy, you were never cut. Nor are you able to change into a bear. It was all him. He only made you think you had been. The violence of the lovemaking would have been real. Hollie would have convinced Ian that he had no part in it. He was playing mind games with the two of you. Terrible ones if you ask me." They both said they agreed with her assessment of it. "As I was explaining, he would have had you finish out his sentencing by having you sign off on the paperwork he said you'd get. The money would never have been given, nor would the amount of magic you were to have received been given to you. Mostly he put enough in your heads so you'd believe it. However, I can see you've been fighting against what was told to you, and the magic is slowly being taken apart. It wasn't much, mind you. Just enough that you'd be able to do a few parlor tricks. Then once you signed the paperwork, he would have taken even that away from you."

"Why us?" She told them she didn't know. They were just in the right place at the wrong time. "What can we do to make it so he never does this again? I'm assuming that since you're here, this is something that Lucy and I have to take care of."

"Yes. That's another thing he'd not counted on—how intelligent the two of you are. Anyone else might have questioned his motives for picking you, but once the magic kicked in, it would have been a walk in the park for him to have gotten them to sign off on his sentencing." Neither of them said anything, but she could tell they were thinking hard on this. "As to what the two of you can do to stop this from happening again, you have to confront him. And you will when—if, I guess I should say—you don't sign the paperwork."

"Oh, you can bet we're not signing shit. The fucker is going to regret trying to bamboozle us." Lucy looked at Ian and laughed. "I think I've been spending a little too much time with your parents. That's one of the things I've picked up from them."

They asked her a great many questions about Hollie.

What had happened to have him in a cell of magic, and so on. But the most important thing they hadn't asked was what they would get out of stopping Hollie. A great many things depended on them doing this. Then there was the reward that would be there for doing a job that was never meant for the two of them to do.

"When you said all we needed to do was confront him about this, I have a feeling it's not as simple as that." She told Ian it was, really. "So, we just tell him he's full of shit, and we're not playing his games? That doesn't sound like it's going to do us much good in the way of stopping him. What is it you're not telling us?"

She laughed. It had been a long time since she'd laughed so hardily. They were going to be the perfect couple for putting a stop to Hollie. More than that, they were going to be the couple that would, in the future, get things done that were needed of them. Nothing so confusing as what Hollie had tried to tell them to do. But it would go a long way in helping humans and creatures alike.

"Confronting him is what you must do. Once his courier comes with the paperwork, you need only to tell them you're not signing anything. That the two of you have had a change of heart. It will, in seconds, bring Hollie back to where you are." Ian eyed her carefully. "He will attack you, Ian. You must be prepared for it. Both of you will need to be on the ready for him to try and harm you. Then, as you said, you would kill him before, one of you must remove his head. As he wronged you and your mate, it can only be one of you who makes sure he's no longer around to harm others. Ending his life is the only sure way to make sure he isn't around any longer."

"I can avenge my mate by removing his head. And what consequences will happen to me for killing a magical being?" She told him that as she was the one in charge of Hollie, she would never press charges against him for defending his mate. "That's it? I can walk away without anyone coming back at me later demanding that I end up in prison for ending the life of a bastard?"

"I promise you, Ian James McCray and Lucy Jackson McCray, on my honor as the mother to all creatures of the earth, that nothing will befall you in any way for you ending the life of Holland."

They stared at her for several minutes. When Ian put out his hand, she took it gladly. Then Lucy did the same. By them shaking on it, the bond to keep the promise to them was as binding as their love for each other.

"Thank you. There are things I will tell you. Once you have removed his head, his body, what will be only ash, will disappear. Don't be alarmed if one of the palace guards comes to you. He is only there to get a sample of the dust, so it can be confirmed that he's dead. Once he is gone, you will be free to live out your life as you wish. The magic you now have, you can keep. However, if you wish to get rid of it at any time, you need only to call for me in the forest, and I will come to you to do so."

She stood up, and the two of them did as well. Gena asked if they had any questions of her. When they both said they didn't at the moment but they might later, Gaea told them she'd be back sometime to make sure they were doing well.

"I've come to enjoy your company. You're a fresh breath of air compared to others I have had to work with. Your ability to say what you think and to make me laugh is something I rarely encounter in my job. I wish to thank you both for this." They shook again. This time she gave them a little magic that would help them to see when the courier was on his way. Being prepared would go a long way in Hollie not being able to talk his way out of the mess he'd made on his own. "Now, I must go. Be careful with Hollie. And good luck."

After she left them, Gaea went to her castle and sat at her desk. There was plenty for her to do, but she sat there thinking about the couple she'd just left. They'd been a great deal more helpful than anyone she'd ever worked with before. Not only that, but she thought they'd do well if she ever needed help again.

The payment they were to receive once Hollie was gone would be great. While she didn't know what its equivalent would be in their world, she knew it was a great deal in hers. Once they had it, she knew even though it was never asked of them, they'd do many things with it that would help others of their kind, humans and shifters alike.

"They have decided to end his life?" She told her mother they would. Mother Nature was someone she loved more than her own spouse at times. "You have gotten their payment gathered, have you?"

"Yes. I had it with me, divided into two different packets, while I was there. But it didn't seem like the time to give it to them. They never asked as you said they wouldn't." Mother

Nature said they were a good family. A better bloodline than she'd ever encountered. "You told me they've done much for us in the past, without so much as a payment from us. This will be good for these two. I believe we'll be able to ask of them again if we have such problems on that side."

"I agree. However, let us just hope they can take care of Hollie. It will be good to know he's been taken out of our lives." Gaea agreed. "When are you planning to go back and pay them? Soon, I hope."

"I'm not going there to give them the payment. I think there would be a fight should I be there when it arrives." Mother Nature laughed and told her she was more than likely right. "I know I am. I will make sure they're compensated, but I shall send others when they call for me to explain. They'll get used to it, I think. And work with it to help everyone as well."

"I think you're right." Nodding, Mother Nature left her. Just as she got to the door, she turned back. "I've given them some magic as well. Enough to ensure they can care for themselves and others. They are, as I said, a good strong family."

Gaea knew that as well and put all the funds that were to be theirs into a package. It would have to be delivered soon, but not before they confronted Hollie. The couple might well back out if she did it beforehand.

Chapter 9

Lucy was elbow deep in a batch of dough when her sisters joined her. They'd been spending a lot of time at their new grandparents' house, and she was sure they were having more fun than they'd been having here with her. Jilly had gotten her driver's license a couple of days ago and had been driving everywhere they had to go. She'd been really good about taking her sister with her too. The two of them seemed to be closer than ever.

"When are you going to open?" Lucy told Cybill they were going to have a soft opening tomorrow. That was what she was doing here tonight. "I don't know what that means. But whatever it does, can I come in and help out?"

"For a soft opening, it means we're going to just open up and not advertise that we are. Hopefully, we'll learn a few things, so when we have a grand opening, advertised this time, we'll have all the bugs worked out." Lucy wiped her hands off after cleaning the dough off them. "Yes, you can help tomorrow. I'm hoping to have a few trays of sliced bread around, as well as some of the cookies we'll be selling once we're open. I'm just playing it by ear for now. However, if you would like to help with the upkeep on them, I'd appreciate it. And if you want to get some work time in tonight, you can help with the decoration of the cookies I've baked."

Jilly was moving around the place like she was casing the joint, as Ian would say. When Lucy asked Cybill what was going on, she just shrugged. She and her baby sister talked about the trays she was putting together, as well as the little pots of butter and jelly to put on them.

"Can I have a full-time job? Not here, but one I can work at every day?" Lucy asked Jilly about school. "I've not told you yet, but I got my test results back. I've tested out of the rest of my high school grades and can skip a few college classes. I want to work before I go to college full time."

"That's wonderful, Jilly! Why didn't you tell us?" She shrugged and said it wasn't that big of a deal. "Of course, it is. It would have been to Ian as well. We should celebrate."

"No. Please don't. I don't want people to think I'm a nerd. I like studying. And because you helped me while we were homeless, I did a lot better than I might have done if you hadn't. No, I don't want to celebrate right now. When I graduate from college, that'll be good." Lucy was disappointed, but only told Jilly she understood. "I have some things I'd like to talk to you and Ian about too. It's about me working. I've been helping out Melody on a couple of things she's doing now, and I'd like to work with her. She said I had to ask you and

Ian. Did you know she's going to be building doors and other safety projects for schools all over the world?"

"I did, as a matter of fact. Her brother, he's working with her too." Jilly said she'd been learning how to use a couple of tools that Melody had. "I don't have to tell you to be careful, do I? I'm sure Melody knows you're just learning."

"She does. I have to wear all the safety gear she wears when she works. When you think you can't be hurt by what you're using, then you're going to kill yourself, Melody told me. I believe her. Getting cocky about them will also get you killed." Lucy wanted to ask what had happened to have that comment come up, but she knew she'd have to trust Jilly's judgment on this. She was almost an adult now. "I've been really careful. Then today, she paid me. My first paycheck and it was for over five hundred dollars. I was shocked about it. But Melody told me I was saving her a lot of time and energy by being careful and doing the little jobs she hates. Can I work for her?"

"I'd say you already are, Jilly." Her cheeks turned bright pink. "I don't have a problem with you working for her so long as you do a few things for me. It's not much, I promise you, but would you take a college class, just one each quarter, to keep your head in the game? It doesn't have to be anything that will take you away from working, but something that will keep your mind stimulated. Also, I'd like for you to save at least half your paycheck. The rest you can blow if you want, but you should put some of it away for later. You might want to buy a house or a new car."

"All right. That's what Melody told me too. You two must

have great minds and all. But she told me that saving money is what makes people money. Also, she said I should have Demi invest it for me." That was much too easy, but Lucy didn't comment. "Ian said I'd have to talk to you about this. He came into the place where we were working and asked me what the hell I thought I was doing. He wasn't mad or anything. Just shocked, I think. After I told him what was going on, he told me he was disappointed in me for not telling at least you about my grades. To be honest with you, Lucy, it never occurred to me. You've been so busy here, and I've been trying so hard to fit in that I just wanted to move on to the next phase. I didn't mean to hurt you."

"I'm glad you told me. And I'm not hurt." She realized she really wasn't. Just shocked, Lucy supposed. "Have you looked into what it would take for you to not have to go to school? I mean, you're not eighteen yet, so there might be rules."

"I didn't look into that. No. Honestly, I never thought about that part. But I will. I'd like for this to work." Lucy told her she would as well if that was what she wanted. "I really do. This is just something I thought of. How do I open myself an account at the bank? I mean, I'd like to not have money on me all the time. I might be too tempted to spend it."

Cybill spoke up then. "That would be me. Can I have an account too? I mean, you're going to pay me for working, right?"

It was almost too much for Lucy to think about. Mostly it was the fact that her sisters weren't children anymore. And that they were old enough to have jobs and money to spend.

She told her, of course, she'd pay her.

"Good. I have to go to school, but that doesn't mean I can't have a little job, right, Lucy?"

"Yes, I don't see any reason for you not to have a job. So long as your grades are kept up, and you're not working when you should be studying." Cybill said she'd not do that. She liked being smart way more than Jilly did. "You're both very smart. Tomorrow I'll have Ian go with you to the bank. I have to be here."

"No. Not tomorrow. We want to be here for your very first day." She couldn't have been more proud of them than she was at that moment. Jilly asked what she could do tonight. "So you won't have to stay so late and can take us to dinner. By the way, Ian said to tell you he's been notified about the paperwork. That he'll talk to you when you're finished here."

So they'd gotten around to contacting them. Good. The sooner they got this over with, the better she'd feel. Lucy knew Ian felt the same way. It really only had been the one whole day, but waiting for something to happen wasn't something she was all that good at. Confronting someone had never sounded better to her, either. Then she was going to deal with her uncle. He was next on her list of shitheads.

After telling them what else she needed to have done, both of them began working for her. Jilly was enjoying slicing the bread she'd already gotten done, and Cybill was putting the cookies she'd baked two days ago on trays to put on the counter to be iced. Cindy was coming over later to figure out what sort of things she'd need for sandwiches, and that would make the first day as ready as they could be. Jilly even recommended she set up the coffee machine to start brewing when they were about to open.

"We need a sort of tip jar for the two of you." Jilly asked her what she meant. "There will be no charge for what people are snacking on or eating tomorrow. They can tip you for helping with their food and such, but there won't be a bill for the snack food. Loaves of bread, yes. Even more than a dozen cookies. But not for the things that are going to be given to them to try. It's going to be a free day to see what sells and what doesn't. I hope at least half of what I've been making is gotten rid of. I don't want to have tons of bread, cookies, and muffins getting stale."

The tables and chairs had been set up just this morning. There was also a patio next door that people could use. Pretty umbrellas were on each of the tables, as well as some lovely floral decorations in the walk in to decorate the tables in the morning. Those had been donated, along with the huge gift basket that was going to be given away tomorrow night. Lucy told the girls about how it had come about.

"I was putting the curtains on the windows to the back when a nice lady from the jelly shop came by to ask if she could donate a few jars of her merchandise to be used on the bread. I was thrilled, and then about ten more people came over the rest of the day with little bits of things to have here. It was Demi that decided we needed a basket to give away. Then everyone started bringing stuff to put in it. I think it might have about five hundred bucks worth of things in it. Plus, a gift certificate from here for a hundred dollars' worth of bread and other things we'll have." Jilly was looking it over when Ian joined them. "I was just telling them about working tomorrow."

"Great. I'm so glad things are working out here. It'll be a smash hit, I know it." He asked if Jilly had spoken to her about college. When she told him she had, he was all smiles. "I wanted to grab her up and hug her to pieces, but she didn't want that. What kid doesn't want to celebrate an accomplishment like that?"

"My sisters. They're very low key about things." They both laughed when Jilly and Cybill started yelling at each other about something in the back room. "What brings you here? I'm going to meet you later for the confrontation, right?"

"It's sooner than I thought. The man is on his way to our house. He didn't call or anything, but I could feel it like you'd entered the room. I was wondering if you could come back with me now." She said she could, but would have to return. "I'll even help you when we come back. I just want this finished."

"I do too. Yes, we can go. What about the girls? Should they be around?"

He asked them if they wanted to go home. He told them they'd be back for dinner. They both decided to hang out here and finish off the cookies that still needed to be decorated. Mostly it was just putting icing on them and a few sprinkles, and Lucy was sure they could handle that. After they told them where they were going, the two of them sat at the big table and started working. Ian made sure they were locked in, and that one member of his family was close enough if they were needed. She wouldn't have thought of calling a family member to come by. Lucy thanked her lucky heart every time he protected the three of them.

The house was lit up when they got there. It was funny. Now that she was here, she could feel him coming too. He was about a half-mile away. When Hinkley asked if there would be tea or scones needed, Lucy started to tell him, no, but Ian said they would make him as welcome as they would anyone.

"That way, he won't know what hit him when we tell him to hit the road." The doorbell rang as they were both laughing. Hinkley told them to have a seat in the living room, and he'd bring the man to them. "Right. We want to make sure he's as comfortable as we can make him."

They'd spoken to the family about what was going on. No one was more disappointed about what had been done to them than his parents. The grandchild hadn't been real, and Lucy thought that hurt them the most. Ian promised his parents he'd work on it for them. They had been too. It was a lot of fun making a baby.

"Sir, my lady. A Mr. Potter is here to see you. Shall I bring in refreshments?" Lucy told Hinkley, yes, and Mr. Potter sat in the chair across from them. "I have things set up for you in the dining room. There will be more room in there for your work, I believe."

Thanking Hinkley, the three of them made their way to the dining room. Mr. Shoe was there, as well as Ian's parents. Surprised but hiding it well, the three of them sat down with them as they enjoyed scones and tea. Mr. Shoe said he was just a friend of the family, and loved having a little pick me up of the delicious scones Lucy had baked just that morning.

"Did you hear they're opening a bakery? My goodness, I'll have to take up walking more if I have to eat there more than once a day."

Lucy was sort of confused about that since she knew Mr. Shoe was a vampire of some considerable age. However, when he winked at her, she smiled back. Things were moving right along when Mr. Potter pulled out the paperwork he'd brought for his client, the bear.

~*~

Ian listened to Mr. Potter tell them what was on each page of the contract. Ian would lay it aside when he was handed it as if he were satisfied with what he'd been told. There were more sheets to the contract than he'd thought there would be, but it mattered little to him. Ian and Lucy both were going to read each and every word of the paperwork when this was finished.

"Now. Do you understand what it is I've told you?" They both nodded, sure they understood what he said. But that wasn't going to be the end of it. "Good. Good. All you need to do is sign right here on the pages where they're marked for me, and I'll be on my way."

"There wasn't any mention of the pay we're to get." Mr. Potter looked confused for a moment and acted as if he, too, was surprised to learn that. "Also, it says we're to receive magic. What sort of magic is that? I mean, will it be useful in the job Ian's late uncle wants us to do?"

"Yes. Oh yes. It will be useful in the job he's asked you to do for him." There was something there. A tone or wording that Ian had to think about for a second: once he had it, he asked the man. "What do you mean, what's the difference between what he's asked you to do and what the magic will be used for? I do believe they're one and the same."

"You believe that? Or do you know that?" The man was getting frustrated with him. Ian didn't care. However, it looked as if Mr. Shoe was having a hard time keeping a straight face. "I want things clear before we sign this. In fact, now that you've gone over each of the pages, I'm going to read them over. I don't want anything to come up as a surprise when this is finished."

"Read them? My goodness, Mr. McCray. That will take most of the day to do. I don't have time for that." Ian stacked the paperwork up and handed it out to Mr. Potter. "You had an agreement with Mr. McCray. You're going to upset him if you don't believe in him. My goodness. I have gone over each page with you. That should be more than enough, I'd think."

"Perhaps it might be for some people, but not for us." He looked at the clock on the wall. "How about you leave the paperwork here and Lucy, and I will go over it today and tomorrow? Then we'll have our attorney go over it—you know, just to make sure we're all on the same page with the way things are going. Then you can pick them up in a couple of days."

"I will not." Ian just stared at him as the man worked to get his temper under control. "Mr. McCray, I'm sure you can imagine how much my client wants to get on with his life. You delaying things is—"

"His life? But it was my understanding that he was dead and going to the other side. With his family. Isn't that correct?"

Mr. Potter was backtracking when he stood up. "Look. I'm not sure what is going on here, but so far I'm not impressed with what is happening. If he is going on with his life, as you called it, then why are we agreeing to anything? No. I think you'd better just leave things here and let my attorney go over them."

"No." His voice was loud. Mr. Potter was no longer trying to control his mouth or his temper. "Now, you see here. I've gone over things for you, and you're to sign off on them or else I'll have to contact Mr. McCray and tell him you've changed your mind."

"I have." Mr. Potter sat down, then stood up again. He was putting his things into his briefcase as he mumbled about stupid people. "You're leaving?"

"I am. And don't you dare be surprised when Mr. McCray shows up here demanding to know why you've wasted my time today." Ian didn't say anything. "I'm leaving. You will have to deal with him when he arrives. And he will. You can bet on that."

Before Mr. Potter could gather up the contract Lucy was keeping from him, the front door slammed against the wall, not only smashing the wall behind it but also knocking several pictures to the floor. When Hollie walked into the room as his bear, Ian stood up and shifted. Lucy was going to deal with him just the way they'd planned it.

"So you've returned, have you? Shift. Now." Hollie turned to his male self and tried in vain to cover himself up. Lucy tossed a small napkin at him, and he was able to hide his cock from her. "You're nothing but a lying piece of shit, and

I'm here to make sure you get your comeuppance."

"I've only come here to see if I could answer any questions for you. It seems as if you've changed your mind. No trouble. I'll just have to find some other maiden and mate to do this job for all the others in the—" Lucy told him to shut his mouth. "This is no way to talk to your elders, young lady. You'll sit yourself down and be quiet while I speak to your mate."

"I said to shut that flapping trap of yours before I remove it from your face. I'm going to do the talking right now, and you're going to pay attention. You hurt me. For no other reason than you thought you could lie your way out of prison and have someone else take over your sentence. Why you thought you could dupe the two of us is beyond me. You've met your match in me, you overgrown horse's ass." Ian laughed a little, and Lucy put her hand on his head. He also noticed his parents were still eating their scones, and Mr. Shoe was watching the event unfold. "I said to sit your ass down."

He did so then. Hollie looked as confused by that as Mr. Potter did. Lucy asked his dad to keep an eye on Mr. Potter as he tried to shimmy his way to the door without anyone noticing. As soon as he was brought into the room, Dad put him in the chair next to his and put a hand on his shoulder. When he shifted it to his large claw, Mr. Potter not only bled a little but whimpered as well.

"I've been in contact with Gaea. You remember her, don't you? She's the one that sentenced you to prison for the rest of your life?" When he didn't answer her, Lucy demanded that he did. "If you think I'm fucking around with you, then you're sadly mistaken. Answer me, you cock sucker."

Mom cleared her throat, and he saw Lucy wink at her. Things were going to come to a head in a little while, and he hoped his mom was going to be all right with it. He was. Ian had cleared his head and heart of any good feelings for this man when he'd been told what kind of person this Hollie was.

"As is my right as the injured party, I hereby ask that you are sentenced to death." Hollie stood up, and Ian growled. His dad did the same. No one moved when he sat back down. Then Mr. Shoe patted Lucy on the back and told her he had this. "He injured me, Mr. Shoe. I don't want you to get into trouble for this."

"I won't. You might say that Gaea and I have ourselves a little understanding." He looked at Ian, then smiled. "Ian, if you would allow me to avenge your wife, I will gladly do so with no stipulations on it. I will end this man's life for the sole reason that he had the nerve to think you would fall for his ploy."

"I don't know what you're talking about. I'm going home." Mr. Shoe turned and looked at Hollie when he stood up. That was all it took for the naked bear to take his seat again. "This isn't right. I've done nothing at all wrong, and I will not be harmed in any way. I've changed my mind about you, Ian. You're not a fit person to be caring for the lands I'm leaving behind."

"Lands? You said nothing about lands." Lucy looked at Ian. "Did he mention lands when he was telling us how we were going to be taking care of the bear population? Did he say anything about it when we were being told about the magic we'd receive? That he'd changed me into a bear or that

I was having a child? I don't remember any mention of lands. Do you?"

Lucy turned back to Hollie. Ian couldn't see her face, but he could almost taste the tension in her body. As Mr. Shoe spoke again, Ian watched Hollie. The man moved—not a lot, but enough to put him on his guard. As soon as he moved the second time, Lucy leapt at the other bear.

~*~

Sitting as still as she could, Lucy didn't look around the room. She didn't want to make eye contact with anyone just yet. Nor did she want to look at the area that was, quite frankly, covered in blood. When Ian came back from upstairs, having been given permission to shift and dress, she took his hand like a lifeline.

"It's going to be all right." Lucy glared at him. "Honey, I'm not trying to upset you, but you're hurting my hand. Please allow me to have some blood to go my fingers."

She let go of him but took his hand back after he shook his hand and kissed the back of hers. Gaea and another woman moved by her again, but she didn't look at them. It was hard enough, she thought, knowing she'd been lied to about a great many things. Hollie was dead. Knowing that was making things like the lies a little easier to swallow.

"You well enough to speak to me now, Lady Lucy?" She told the voice no. That she didn't want to talk to anyone ever again. "I don't think that is even remotely possible, do you? My dear, it will only take a moment for me to release you from your own hell. You did the right thing in killing him."

"You said I wasn't a bear." The woman got down on the

floor next to Ian. It was impossible not to see her now. She thought someone said she was Mother Nature, but in her mind, there wasn't a real Mother Nature. Was there? "Gaea said that I wasn't a bear. She told me I had been tricked. She lied to me too."

"You're not bear." Lucy asked her what the fuck she was talking about. "You're not. I don't know where the magic came from that allowed you to shift your hand into a claw and take off Hollie's head, but I'm ever so grateful he didn't hurt you. Aren't you?"

"That's not the point." The woman, she still didn't know her name for sure, told her it was. "I'll decide what makes my point and doesn't."

"Lucy? You're not making any sense." She knew that too but didn't appreciate Ian pointing it out. So she kicked him in the leg. "Yes, that's the perfect way to win an argument. Kicking me while I'm down. You saved us both, love. Had you not moved and killed him when you did, he would have killed Mr. Shoe and myself. I didn't know that he had a silver stake on his person when he was naked. I'm sure no one would have thought to check his back for them either."

"Why?" Ian asked her what she meant. "Why was I able to kill him the way I did? I'm not bear. That's been pointed out to me numerous times already."

"I can answer that if you'd not mind." Everyone turned to Gaea. She smiled at them. "Mr. Shoe did it. When he touched you, he gave you the power to end the man's life in any fashion you needed. He told me to tell you both when you finished feeling sorry for yourself. I think he thought it might take you a bit longer to get around to questioning how it happened. But he's very powerful. More so than I think even I realized."

"I'm going to have to reward the man." The woman spoke from the floor, and that was when Lucy looked at her. Really stared at her. "You know me, Lucy. I've been with you before. When you were caring for your sisters."

"You were a homeless woman." The woman nodded. "You told me you knew where I could get hot food. Where I could get enough for my sisters and myself. That was where I met the McCrays. You planned this, didn't you? Who are you?"

"Mother Nature." Lucy wondered if she thought her joke was funny. She certainly didn't think it was. "I am, child. Mother Nature. Gaea is one of my daughters, one of many that helps me keep things in check. I saw you struggling and decided you'd be the perfect bride for one of the McCray men. I had no idea Ian would be the one. But having you in this family is going to mean great things for a lot of people. Like the idea you have for the homeless."

Her face heated up when she mentioned her unspoken idea. Ian asked her what it was. She told him she'd go over it with him when they got home.

"We are home, love. Tell me." She explained what she wanted to do. His face told her he loved the idea. "Giving the homeless a time to come in and get warm in the winter months by working for you is an excellent idea. I love you're going to make sure all the leftovers are donated to the local charities to use. You're a very smart cookie, have I told you that lately?"

"No, no one has ever said that to me." She hugged him when he stood up and pulled her from the chair. "I killed a man, Ian. I don't know what to do about that."

"Nothing. Nothing at all. He did harm you. And he would have killed me too if you'd not reacted faster than me." Ian lifted her chin up, and she saw his love for her in his eyes. "You saved my life and that of Mr. Shoe. He's gone home now to rest. He said he'd return when things were calmed down, and he'd give you his gift. I'd not turn it down if I were you either. Demi said he means to give it to you."

"I killed a man, and I don't want to be rewarded for it." Ian kissed her. "I want a child with you, Ian. Please? Let's work on that as soon as we can. I want to hold your child in my arms."

"I'd like nothing better. Yes, we'll work on that as much as we possibly can." When he wiggled his brows at her, she laughed. It didn't hurt her as much as she thought it would. Laughing after killing a man. "I've sent for your sisters. They've finished up the cookies and are headed home. Thanks for bringing them into my life as well."

Chapter 10

Josh didn't know what to do about his face. Yesterday he'd walked out of the hospital when they told him they couldn't do anything else for him. What they were telling him, in their sly way, was that he was going to have to live with his face looking like a train wreck. Also, they weren't going to help him with any more surgeries because he was as fixed as he could be. The doctor had actually told him he had to heal before he could be operated on again. He didn't want to *heal*, looking like this. Every time he looked in the mirror, it made his belly sick. Josh didn't want to be fixed later either, damn it. It needed to be perfect, as he'd been before this bullshit.

Last night he'd spent in an old barn with more holes in the roof than not. It took him nearly an hour to find a place that wasn't dripping water on his head. Then longer than that to find a place not soaked with mud. Lying on a bed of straw wasn't as comfy as it was made to look on the television either. All sexy and shit wasn't happening.

There hadn't been a bit of food for him. Not that he expected someone to find him and feed him, but it would have been nice if he'd been given some money upon leaving the hospital. He told them to charge it to his nieces, but they said they were not a bank and didn't work like that. Fuckers. Every last one of them.

He'd been walking around since the farmer or whatever the hell he'd been walked into the barn and found him sleeping next to his tractor. There was no dealing with some people, Josh had discovered. The man didn't give a shit about it being the only place in the barn to rest. Josh was chased out of the place with a huge sharp devil-like pitchfork.

There wasn't any humanity in the world anymore. People were out for only one thing, and that was whatever they wanted. Josh was the same way, he knew that, but his had been just cheating his family. Not the rest of the world. Someone should have thought of that too. Josh wasn't a horrible person to everyone. Just family. If more people were like that, they'd not have all these other things going on.

He'd seen the two younger girls of his brothers several times over the last few hours. They wouldn't have shit on them to steal, so he left them alone. It was the only reason he'd not bothered them. Once he thought about just kidnapping one or both of them, but he knew for some reason, he wasn't up for keeping them. They'd hurt him. Josh wasn't going to get himself hurt any more than he had to. They'd go for his face too, he just knew it.

A lovely scent made its way to him. He knew the smell—

bread. Fresh from the oven. His mom used to bake bread when she was upset. It seemed toward the end of her life she would be caught baking every day. He, mostly, was the cause of it. Not that he really cared, but Josh knew he'd not been the easiest kid to raise.

Donald had been easy. Of course, he was Mom's favorite because of that. He didn't get into trouble, never had a bad grade, nor did he cheat on things like tests or girlfriends. Not that he was nice. Donald did have a reputation for being somewhat of a prick at times. Then after he and Lucille were married, the two of them seemed to live for doing shit that involved them traveling a great deal. Also, not sharing their good times with him. Not even having children slowed them down. Most of the time, he found out, they left the kids at home, in the care of the household. Who did that to kids?

He would have, he realized in a heartbeat. Josh thought that he'd have left them on the doorstep of some unsuspecting neighbor, so he didn't have to spend any time with kids. Not that his nieces were all that bad, but damn, they could make a man wish he'd opted out of having anything to do with them. Girls whined and moaned about every little thing he did.

The television was too loud for them to sleep. Christ, then sleep in another room, he'd told them. There wasn't any food in the house. Because he'd gotten to the point of hiding it in the room with him. And he told the staff not to purchase anything that he didn't approve of. He knew they had. The girls seemed to be just fine while they lived there. But he had griefs too, damn it.

The hot water would forever be out when it was his turn

to use his shower. It seemed to him they were draining the fucking hot water tank just to piss him off. Also, the rooms that he'd claimed as his own were not being cleaned up. Even when he ordered the fucking staff to do it, he'd come into the room with it looking just the way it had when he left it. The staff was fucking with him. But he couldn't fire them. He needed them to answer phone calls and get the mail. About all they were good for.

At first, he would share his food with the girls. But what he bought was never right. Why did they have to have different things for meals other than just pizza? It didn't satisfy them with him buying meat pizzas, veggie ones, as well as just cheese. That didn't go over well, so he stopped trying. Nor did they like that he never bought juice or milk. Mother fuck, it was like he was living with a bunch of Donalds, and he had enough.

Lucy was the worst of the three of them. She would come into his office and demand that he take care of things. Like the bills her parents had incurred. Why the hell should he be responsible for his brother's bills? Then she wanted to see the will.

"I don't think you're going to be able to understand it." She told him if he could, she'd not have any trouble. "Don't be a bitch, Lucy. You're just lucky I'm allowing you to live here. You and your sisters are going to do what I want, or I'm going to show you the back of my door."

"It's the back of your hand, moron." Lucy told him she wanted him to hand over his copy of the will. "I want to make sure you're really here to care for my sisters. I have no idea why anyone would think you'd be a good choice to keep an eye on two little girls."

"You're mentioned in the will for me to take care of too." She told him she was an adult and hadn't lived at home for years. "So? You think that mattered to your parents? It didn't. I'm your only living relative, and what I say goes. You'd better get used to that, or I'll set you out of the house once and for all."

Three days later, he did just that. Lying to them had become a fun pastime. But they were catching on to him faster than he could come up with a plausible lie. He dropped them off at the mall, telling them he had to get some cash from the bank, then he was going to take them out to dinner. He'd had a fine steak dinner that night, while they— Well, he had no idea what they had, and didn't give a good fuck either. So long as they were out of the house.

"Hello, Josh." He turned and looked at the man standing in front of the bakery shop he'd been looking into. He didn't know who he was, but he did look like someone he might well have hung out with. Money. The man had it to spare too. "You don't know me, do you? I'm hurt."

"I'm sorry, buddy, but it's been a long time, hasn't it? Tell me who you are over a couple of nice dinners, and we'll catch up." The man laughed. "Yes, it's a funny world we live in now, don't you think?"

"It is. Even funnier if you think I'd buy you dinner for not knowing me. I'm Lucy's husband, Ian McCray. You remember me now, don't you? I'm sure you do every time you look in the mirror. You're a piece of shit." He told the man he was rude. "Rude? I guess that's your opinion. However, I think you're a piece of shit. Leaving helpless, defenseless girls out on the streets while you live it up in their family home. Shame on you."

Josh laughed. "That's the best you can do? Shame on me? Here I thought you were this great big bear that was going to teach me a lesson. Well, for your information, you're going to get billed for what you did to me. Look at this shit. I'm going to have to live with this for the rest of my life, thanks to you." Ian told him he didn't care. "You'd better care. Because when I'm finished with those girls, I'm going to come after you."

Ian just walked away, laughing. Josh couldn't stand to be laughed at, but it was worse when someone walked away from him when he still had things to say. Just as he was coming up behind the man, to do what he wasn't sure, he got a slight pain in his face that reminded him what had happened to him the last time he'd tangled with the prick.

Then he saw her. Jilly. Christ, she'd grown up over the last few weeks. Looking at her now, he couldn't believe he'd let this one get away. He could have made some major bucks off her—even the younger one. Seeing them there together, their heads close, talking about who cared what, Josh tried to think what was the best way to get them back to the house where he could get some serious bucks off them.

"Touch them, and I'll never even think about what I did to you." He looked at the very large woman that was standing beside him. "You might want to rethink a lot of shit that's going through your head right now, Josh. See that woman over there staring at you? She can put you in a world of hurt and not touch you once."

"Are you fucking with me right now? You're so big I'd have trouble getting my dick in you. The other one? Well, she's just as happy as a pincushion sitting over there. I doubt she's even aware we're talking about her." She asked him if he was referring to his tiny prick. "Listen here, bitch. I'm not tiny at all. I have women all over the world, talking about my sexual manliness."

He'd not meant to say that. Hell, he'd not even meant to engage with her. But her laughter had him reaching for her. Just as his hand grabbed for her, she moved in a way that left him with a handful of air. Then he found himself on his back with a foot at his throat. The woman sure could move fast for as fat as she was. Then a man, another one of them fucking bears, came into his view.

"You thinking of cutting me up too, mister?" The man said he thought his wife had it just fine. "You're going to let the little woman—or I should say, fat slob—take care of me? Wow, are you pussy whipped."

"Nope. Just a man who knows his wife is more badass than he could ever hope to be. But my *manliness,* as you called yours, is all right with her being the one wearing the pants." The man laughed. "She's not fat, either, but carrying our child. How does it feel to be taken down by a pregnant woman?"

"Sure, she's fat. Just look at her. Who would want to fuck that thing?" The pain in his head had him closing his eyes against the sudden and very real thought that his head had been split open like a melon. "What the fuck did you do to me?"

"Hit you. Christ, you are a pussy, aren't you?" Josh just laid there, and when someone said his name, he looked up to find the woman from across the street standing over him. The man, he didn't remember his name, spoke again. "This is my sister-in-law, Meadow. She is going to talk to you for a little while, then you're going to go away. If not, I get to kick your ass. Either way, you're not going to be hanging around here for much longer."

Josh was helped up from the ground. He didn't know where he was, but it certainly wasn't anywhere he'd been before. He looked at the woman, Meadow, and asked her what was going on. All she did was smile at him and ask him to have a seat. The chair, which hadn't been there before, hit him behind his legs and he had no choice but to sit.

"I'm not anyone you want to fuck with. You might call me dangerous. I think I'm just lucky. You see, I can manipulate your mind into seeing all sorts of things that aren't there. Like this." The dragon blew fire all over him, and he screamed as he tried to put the fires out. Christ, he was burning up from head to toe. "He's gone."

Josh sat there for several minutes, not moving. Taking an inventory of his body, he realized that not only was he not burned to a crispy fry, but his clothing was all right too. Meadow was still smiling at him when he asked her what she wanted.

"Nothing. I mean, I want all sorts of things that I'm not going to get, like a big chocolate malt. I so love them over milkshakes. But I promised I'd stay here for this first opening of the Gathering Place. Then you had to come along and mess it up, didn't you?" He asked her what she was talking about. "The shop that Lucy is making her own. The girls are working here as well. It's been a very successful day for the three of them. And after this, Jilly is going to be working for my other sister, Melody. You'd not like her any more than you will me. Why are you even alive?"

"That's a stupid question. I'm alive because I was born. Why are you even here? If the girls are working, then why are they taking all my money from me?" She told him it wasn't his money in the first place. "Sure, it is. My brother left it all to me."

"No, he didn't. He left you nothing because you were nothing to him. Especially after you tried to rape his wife." Josh told her no one knew that. "Lucille did. She told her husband after it happened. That was when they not only changed their will regarding you, but also made it so you could never enter their home or be around them or their daughters."

"I told her not to say anything. It's not like I got anything from her anyway. She told me she didn't want me, and I walked away." Lies, she told him. Meadow just shook her head as he tried to cover up what should never have been spoken about. "Why would that bother him so much? I mean, seriously. It was just something between her and I. I don't understand women. She put a wedge between us, and I'm glad she's dead now."

The room shifted. It was like being in a fast moving car, but instead of driving, they were rolling over and over. When it came to a sudden stop, it took Josh a few seconds to get his bearings. When he did, he realized that somehow they were in the kitchen of his brother's home, and Lucille was there with him. It was the day he'd tried to get her to let him fuck her.

~*~

Lucy held onto Meadow's hand as she spoke to Josh. She could see what Josh did. Hear his voice, and also feel when he was lying. It was the strangest thing she'd ever witnessed. As they moved through his memories, Lucy saw things Josh had done in the name of being their uncle that she'd never dreamed of a human doing to one of their kin. She looked at her mother and saw how bruised and beaten she was.

"You come near me again, and I'll kill you." Josh laughed at her mom when she threatened him. "You mother fucker, you tried to rape me. Why would you even think I'd want anything sexual to do with you?"

"Because I'm a better lover than my brother? There are all kinds of reasons why. But I didn't go through with it, so you don't have anything to say to Donald." Mother put a wet washcloth to her face, then rinsed out the blood she'd wiped off. "If you tell my brother, Lucille dear, the next time I won't stop."

"You only stopped this time because I beat you. The next time you try anything, I'll be carrying a gun. You can bet on that." Josh just laughed at her mother. "You just wait and see, Josh. I'm going to tell Donald, and he'll make sure you're barred from ever coming here again."

He grabbed her around the throat and held her there. "You tell my brother, and I'll kill you and those girls of yours. What will he do then? Who do you think he'll believe?"

Mother kicked him in the balls, and Josh went flying back. When he landed on the floor, Mother picked up a large skillet and hit him several times on the head with it. Seeing that he wasn't moving, Lucy figured, her mother calmly laid the skillet down and called for help. Mr. Morse, the butler, then came and helped Mother drag Josh out of the house, and set him by the trash cans.

"Did your mother carry a gun after that?" Lucy told Meadow she had, even if they were only going to a neighbor's. "This man should have been killed long ago, I think. I know I'd be happier if he was dead."

Lucy looked at Josh as he watched the memory Meadow had gotten from his mind. The smile on his face sickened her. He'd hurt her mother. And in turn, he'd hurt his own brother. She had wondered for a long time what had happened between the three of them that caused Josh to stop coming around. Now she knew. And she hated him all the more for it.

The memories were raced over again. She knew this one was more recent. She was living at home with her sisters then. The dress she had on was something she had only gotten to wear the one time before being tossed out of their family home.

"What the fuck is going on in here?" Jilly was just out of the shower, and the two other girls were in her room. "Get out of here. I don't know what you're planning, but you can just forget it right now. I'm not leaving. I'm in charge of the three of you, and you'll begin to listen when I speak. Go to your rooms."

Jilly had tried to go with Lucy. Even then, it had seemed

strange to her how much she hated Josh. But as soon as the door closed behind them, he went to it and locked it. Lucy felt her skin crawl when she realized what Josh was going to do.

"Jilly, you and I have some unfinished business, I think." She told him to get out of her room. "I don't think so. You're going to help me out with my little problem, or I'm going to have to get it from someone else. Like your little sister. Do you think Cybill will be any good at letting me fuck her?"

"You touch her, and I'll kill you. And I'm not going to help you with your problem either. You come near me again, and I'm going to hurt you in ways that the little problem you have now will never bother you again. I'm going to rip it off and make you eat it, you fucking bastard." This was a side of her sister she'd never seen. Lucy was very proud of her. "Get out of here."

Jilly grabbed her hairspray and a lighter. It took her a second to realize what she was up to when a flame shot out of the bottle towards Josh. Him jumping back, screaming at her to behave, had her laughing. Even Meadow was impressed, cheering her sister on as if she was right there with her.

"Where are you getting this shit? I know for a fact she never told anyone about this." Meadow asked Josh how he could be so sure. "Because Lucy would have killed me. Or that bear husband of hers. Jilly should have just put out, and I would have been done with her."

"She's your niece, you fuck head. You do know it's against the law, don't you?" Josh shrugged at Meadow, and that pissed Lucy off more. "Jilly is a great deal like her mother, don't you think? Both of them put you out to the trash, just where you belonged. Someone should have made sure you were picked up, is all. I think the plan for you is to do just that. You're going to be in a world of hurt; you know that, don't you?"

"Me? I think not. As you have so nicely pointed out, nothing ever happened between the three of us." Josh smiled at Meadow, still having no idea Lucy was there with him in his memories. "I was just thinking about how wonderful it would have been to have Jilly and her mother at the same time. Holy Christ, I would have had that several times before I was put out. They would have enjoyed it too."

Letting go of Meadow also meant Lucy let go of the memories of Josh. At this point, she didn't care. Hitting him or killing him won out over seeing any more of his sick thoughts. As soon as she touched him, Josh looked at her, surprised. Lucy had no problem knocking that look right off his face and him onto the ground.

She kicked him several times in the head before someone grabbed her from behind. It didn't stop her from still working on getting to him, but whoever was holding her had a firmer grip than she could break. It was when Ian spoke that she finally calmed down.

"He's not worth you going to jail for." Meadow stood in front of her, and Lucy grabbed her, sobbing out how hurt she was for what she'd seen. "Don't worry about it, Lucy. I promise you, he's going to get what he deserves. Well, not what he deserves, but more like what I think he should be getting. Josh will live for a long time, but his mind will never be the same. I'm going to make sure of that. Killing him would be entirely too easy on him. I think making him suffer will be the best thing for us all."

"You can do that?" Meadow winked at her. "Whatever you want to do to him, then do it. I want him to suffer. My god, he wanted to rape my sister. And my mother." She wanted to kick him again. "Meadow, I will be forever grateful to you and owe you whatever you want if you were to make him suffer. I never knew. I didn't know what sort of monster he was."

"You need to talk to Jilly." She nodded at Ian as he spoke in her ear. "It can wait until we get home today, but as soon as you can arrange it, I'd have a long talk with her about Josh and what he's done. What you know he's done."

"I will. I don't even want to think of what else was in his head about her." Meadow didn't say anything, for which Lucy was grateful. "Do you know if he did anything to Cybill?"

"He didn't. Josh was afraid of her. You have to admit that of the three of you, she's the most outspoken. But after today, I think you might be able to give her a run for her money." The laughter was just what she needed. "I've called the police. They're going to take him to jail, where he'll have a slight episode and have to be sent away to a mental institution. It's the best place for him. And you'll never have to worry about him being set free. I plan on making him see things from my perspective as to how he should have died a long time ago."

Lucy mingled with the people at the shop after Josh was taken away. She wanted to lose herself in the people but was worried about her sister. However, every time she looked at her, Jilly was laughing and having a great time.

There were a great many more that had shown up than she'd thought there would be. The bread had been a great success, she saw. The cookies were also a big hit, and Cybill had asked if they could take orders for them from people. After giving her permission to do so, Lucy wondered how many people would want cookies. Not many, she thought.

Ian was close at hand every time she reached for him. Meadow and the other sisters were waiting on people out on the patio. Even Alden and Cindy seemed to be having a great time talking to the customers. But then, she thought they could have a conversation with anyone and have a good time.

All in all, she thought it was a great success. She was sad for the tip jar, but since her sisters didn't mind that it didn't have anything in it but some change, she wasn't going to worry about it either. Today, Lucy thought, was going to be a good day no matter what came about later.

"Did you see the tip jar?" She told Cybill she was sorry about it. "Why? Oh, wait, you didn't see us. We have emptied it three times, Lucy. Three whole times when it was stuffed to the top. There were fives and even twenties in there. Jilly and I are going to save every penny of it too."

After Cybill walked away, laughing at something only a fifteen-year-old could, Ian came to stand with her again. She asked him about the tip jar. He said he'd been the one that had told them to empty it.

"They're never going to let me charge for food again if they can make this sort of money." They both laughed. "I'm glad they're having such a good time. And they're getting to know some of the other people around town too. That's always a plus."

She didn't want to talk about Josh, and Ian seemed to understand that. As they drifted between people sampling the things she'd baked for today, they talked about bread and other things she thought about making for the shop. There were plenty of ideas too. Everyone seemed to really enjoy the swirl breads with real fruit in them. And the simple sugars cookies that her sisters had decorated. She'd have to tell them how well they'd done.

Making notes on her phone as to the ideas she'd been given, Lucy was ready to start baking right now. By the time everyone was going home, she was ordering supplies she was going to need for her baking. Even when she'd finished with getting all the things she was going to need, Lucy was as excited as she'd ever been. Not even the likelihood of having to clean up a huge mess when she baked curbed her need to get her hands covered in dough and starting to make all the things on her list. She looked at Ian when he said her name.

"Should I put you a cot here in the room with the ovens, or do you think you might make it home once in a while?" She said she wasn't sure. "I thought so. You're looking at the ovens like they're the next best thing. I'm not even sure you looked at me like that before."

"I might if you had a timer on you." They were holding hands and laughing as they headed to the car. Jilly was going to take Cybill to her grandma's, then she was going to hang out with the local pack. She'd found some people her age and was having a good time. "I'm not sure what I should do about Jilly. She seems so adjusted. I think I'll wait until she comes to me to talk. I know they said I should speak to her about it, but I don't think it's necessary yet. She seems so well adjusted. Don't you think?"

"I think you know her best of all. And if that's what you think, then I'm in full agreement with you." She loved this man. "Also, with the house all to ourselves, I think I can help you along with working on our child. What do you think?"

"I love it and you." Ian kissed her, and she thought of the nighty she'd had shipped to her today. She was going to heat up his world as best she could. "Maybe we should have them spend a couple of days with your parents. It might be nice for us to be alone."

Ian said he'd call his parents as soon as he got home.

Lucy was in love. And she was safe. Two things she'd never in her life thought she'd be. In addition to that, her sisters were well cared for and happy. Life couldn't be better if she had plotted it out for herself.

Chapter 11

There were three women in the household, but Becky didn't know any of them. Not that it mattered all that much. She didn't know a great many people. Her momma told her she was sheltered. Whatever that meant, she was okay with it.

Becky had watched as men built a chicken coop two days ago, then later the same day as they filled it with little chicks. What she wouldn't give to hold just one of them for a minute. She'd be really careful with it. Momma would tell her they were too tiny to be held. It didn't stop her from wanting to hold them, but her momma was always right. Yesterday when the chicks had been fed, Becky had tried some of their food. It wasn't something she would do again. It was hard and tasted like corn. She liked corn, but not hard and full of other things.

Becky moved back into the barn when one of the women came out of the house again.

"I know you're out here. I know you're a girl and alone. I

want to help you if you'll allow it." Becky didn't even breathe when the girl spoke. "I have a sandwich for you from my lunch if you want it. I didn't tell anybody I saw you last night. Come out here, and I'll give you some water too."

Becky didn't want to go, but her belly was empty. Emptier than it had been in a long time. With her momma being dead now, there wasn't anybody around to help her get some food. Moving out of the shadows, she saw the younger girl holding out a sandwich. Becky moved closer. Keeping an eye on the house too, she snatched the sandwich away from the girl and ate a huge bite of it.

"Don't eat too quickly, or you'll get sick. I've been hungry like that before. You don't want to throw up the first meal you've had in a while." Becky nodded and tried to make herself slow down. "If you can keep that one down, I have another one for you. And some water, like I promised."

"Why?" The girl told her it was getting cold out, and she didn't want her to be sick. "My momma died a while back. I'm too little to get her to a funeral home. I didn't call the police either. Because — well, I'm afraid of them too. I'm scared that someone will come and get me."

"I can keep you safe and have the police get to your momma. My mom is dead too. My name is Cybill." Becky told her what her first name was, but nothing more. "Who are you hiding from?"

"My dad. Momma said he's been looking for a reason to kill us off since she left him. I got the book too." Becky didn't mean to tell her about the book. Her momma had told her it was the only reason she'd been able to escape the house.

Cybill didn't ask anything more about it, so she didn't tell her. "Can you call my aunts? They might come and get me if somebody was to call them and tell them my momma is gone."

"I can do that." Cybill looked toward the house, then back at her. "I'm the only one home right now. The staff is here, but they're working. If you trust me, I'll take you into the house and up to my room, where you can get a bath and put on some of my clothing. I promise you, I won't tell anyone where you are."

Becky was tempted. It was getting chilly outside. The only warmth she'd been able to get to was the heating light over the chicks. She looked at Cybill and wondered what she'd do if she told her what she knew about her father.

"I don't care who you are, Becky. You've not hurt the chicks, so I know you can be trusted. I don't know why, but that's what I feel. But I want you to be safe and warm. I know just how you're suffering with all this. I told you, we've been where you are now, and I want to help you." Nodding, Becky hoped that Cybill didn't get hurt when her dad found her. "You'll be safe too. I promise you. My family is the best there is."

Getting into the house was much easier than she thought it should have been. But Cybill promised her they were going to be all right as she led her up the stairs to her bedroom. It was a very pretty room. There were pictures on the walls, as well as a set of bunk beds. Becky had wanted bunk beds in her room since she'd seen them at a friend's house. It seemed so long ago now.

"I'm Cybill McCray. I'm going to be sixteen next month. I think having a birthday in October is sort of sad. I can have a party, but it all has to be indoors. No pool or anything like that for me." Becky told her a little about herself. "I know your name. At least I think it's yours. Your father, Peter Hightower. Isn't he being indicted on several charges of racketeering?"

"Yes. Do you want me to leave?" Cybill asked her why she'd think that. "I don't know. When people hear what my name is, they sort of clam up and stop talking to me. My dad, he's had people killed for less. I'm almost ten. I forgot to tell you that."

"I knew you were younger than me. It's fine. All right, tell me where your mom is, and I'll have someone get the police there." After telling her about a barn they'd been staying in, Cybill picked up her cell phone and called someone named Meadow. After closing the connection, Cybill smiled at her. "My Aunt Meadow is this freaking smart woman. All the people in this family are like that. But Aunt Meadow, she knew you were here. She asked that you stay here, and she'll take care that your mom is found, and no one knows who she is until they can get things fixed up. I don't know what that means, but you can trust her."

"I don't trust anyone. My mom said it would get you killed." Cybill said she understood, then showed her where the bathroom was, as well as let her pick out anything she wanted to wear from her closet. "Are you sure about this? I don't want you to get into any trouble. Sneaking around isn't something that will make people trust you. I know because that's what happened to my mom and myself."

"I've never been more sure of anything in my life." The voices coming from the hallway made Becky want to run. Cybill told her it was her aunt Demi and her sister. Things were going to be fine. "I wouldn't lie to you about this. You have my word that things are going to be all right for you. My sister is the nicest person in the world. So are the rest of the family."

Becky held the clothing she'd been given close to her body. They were really loud, the two women, but they didn't seem to be mad at her. After them talking over her head for what seemed hours, she was told to take her shower, and they'd talk when she came out. Becky was torn. Would they turn her over to her dad? She hoped not. Becky didn't want to ever be back with him again.

The shower was heaven. Washing her hair three times was such a treat that she knew she'd have to replace the shampoo after she left. When she finally made herself get out of the stall, she pulled on clothing that smelled wonderful in its freshness, Becky figured they'd tell her to speed up and get finished. However, when she came out of the bathroom, the room was empty.

Going down the long staircase, she could hear the laughter coming from one of the rooms. Following it, she entered a room filled with people. Backing out, Cybill took her hand and brought her all the way into the room and introduced her to her family.

Lucy smiled at her and told her to have a seat. They were all going to help her. Becky didn't know what to think, so she sat but kept her mouth shut. She no more trusted these people than she had her dad. And she was supposed to trust him.

"Your mom has been taken to the hospital, where they'll take care of her for us. She is now only a Jane Doe until we figure out what caused her death, as well as how much your father knows. We'll have a nice quiet funeral for her in a few days for you." Becky started crying at Demi's words. Just having someone be this kind to her was something she'd missed when her momma had passed away. "You stick with us, Becky, and we'll make sure you're taken care of. I've contacted a friend of mine who is going to notify your aunts after we find out what we can from you about them. They're not going to be told anything about you other than you're safe. Can they be trusted to not tell your father anything?"

"They're my great aunts, really. On my mom's side. My aunt Josephine, she's trustworthy. But Momma told me she'd not trust Margaret any further than she could toss her. She thought my momma should have been happy that a man would marry her. Aunt Margie was in love with my dad before he found my momma." Lucy asked her about her mother's death. "My father had people watching us all the time. I mean, we couldn't go to the mall without having three or four people with us. When we were ready to run—we'd been planning it for weeks—she was shot by one of them. I thought it was getting better, but without food and a safe place to stay, she didn't make it."

"I'm so sorry about that." Becky nodded. "I'll have my friend, Mr. Shoe, find your aunt Josephine then. I'll talk to her when he gets me a number. You can tell me where you think she lives when I call him. It might narrow down the search.

But for now, I wanted to ask you about the book. Meadow knows you have it and where it is, but we don't want to take it from you. It's yours, and it's going to remain yours until you trust us enough to share it with us."

"Do you know what the book is?" They all nodded. "My momma only told me it was going to save her life and mine. It got her killed. That's all I know. She told me to protect it, but not to be killed for it. She died trying to leave my father, and I've no one left."

"Don't say that." She looked at Cybill when she spoke. "Don't say you're all alone. We're here for you. And we will be forever if you'll allow us."

"I just want to be safe." It was too much for her, and she started crying. "We've been running and hiding out for so long now. Then every time we got to someplace we felt like we were safe, someone would come along and tell on us or something. I just want my momma back and for things to be normal. I'm so tired of not having food and a shower. It felt so good to be cleaned up."

She knew she wasn't making much in the way of sense. But being held by Cybill while she sobbed out her nonsense was about as good as being held by her momma. Even having all these people around was better than she'd had it in a long time. For some reason she didn't understand, Becky felt really good for a change.

They talked for a long time. Becky was having trouble staying awake, and when Cybill moved off the couch beside her and put a pillow on the seat, Becky laid down and knew she wasn't going to be awake for very long. As sleep settled over her, Becky thanked Cybill for helping her. If she answered her, Becky had no idea.

She'd had the dream before—the one where her father was sitting in his office with his men with him. Neither Becky nor her momma were ever allowed in the room when he was having a meeting. But that day, Becky had been looking for a pencil sharpener and had nearly gotten caught in the room when they entered. Hiding behind the couch against the wall was all she could find to keep from being hurt for intruding.

"Did you get rid of the bodies?" Her father had a loud voice. It was rough too. Momma told her it was because someone had knifed him once in the neck, and it never healed right. "If this comes back to bite me in the ass, I'm going to make sure you remember who is boss."

"I promise you, no one knows where they are." She thought the man's name was Douglas, but she wasn't sure until her father called him that. "There are some things I should tell you, though. I think the police are looking for them now. They asked me a lot of questions when they came to my house."

"The police were at your house? Why am I just now hearing about this, Douglas? You should have told me first thing. You know how much I hate being in the dark about things like this." This was her father's "I'm going to hurt you" voice. He'd used it on her more than once. "What did you tell them? Are they aware of how they were killed?"

"I don't think they know where they are." Father asked the man if he was sure or did he just think so. "They never mentioned that they knew where the bodies were. Just that you had them killed. They wanted me to tell them that. I didn't."

"I don't believe you." She didn't either. The man looked to her like he was sweating bullets. But all she could see was his face, and nothing more from her position behind the couch. "You told them everything, didn't you, Douglas? Do you have any idea how much that is going to cost you?"

The man's head just exploded. Blood and other things that she didn't want to think about were all over the wall behind the man. His head, laying back at an odd angle, seemed to be flooding the floor with his blood.

Becky had her hand over her mouth, or she might have screamed out loud and been shot too. Her father had killed Douglas. Shot a hole in his head with the gun she knew was in his top drawer. As her father spoke to the other men in the office with him, she watched as Douglas was pulled from the chair and put on a big piece of plastic.

The plastic was delivered once a month to the house. She'd never thought about what it was being used for until now. Once a month, a huge shipment would come in and be set in the barn. Becky didn't want to think about the number of bodies that were being wrapped up with it.

She kept herself still until the room was emptied. Even then, she counted to a thousand twice before she thought she could move. Becky was going to go out the back door to this office and never return, she thought. But she couldn't have left her mother. Not for anything.

Her father had made two phone calls about getting someone in to clean up the mess. They were going to arrive by midnight, he told his men, and they were to be out of the house. When she thought she could get up and out of the room, she was nearly to the door when she decided to cover her bottom.

Pulling out her new cell phone, she took several pictures of the dead man. Then she took pictures of the room. As the last picture, she took a picture of the gun that was back in her father's desk. As she was leaving the room, Becky turned back to the dead man.

Becky watched a lot of crime shows. She was looking for some of the people she knew her father had killed on the shows. It never happened so far, but she had learned a great deal from them. Knowing from them that blood could be traced using some kind of light, she decided to take a couple of samples of it and the room for the police, should she ever be brave enough to go to them. Momma had always told her the police were in her father's pocket. She knew what that meant for sure.

After taking a little bit of the blood from the wallpaper, she cut a small corner of the rug and put them in an envelope. Picking up the gun with a tissue, she put it in one of the many tins her father had saved that held money. Run money, he had told her momma. When she decided she might need the money too, Becky took some more of it from the dozen or so tins around the room. Either he'd notice and think the cleaning crew did it, or she'd be dead before her next birthday.

"Where is it?" Opening her eyes when she heard the voice, she looked at Cybill. The room was dark now, but there wasn't anyone else around. "You talk in your sleep. If you tell me where the money and gun are, I'll have my sister get it for you to keep."

"In the barn where my mom was." Cybill nodded and stood up. "Are you going there now?"

"No. You and I are going to have supper. I waited for you. My sister, Jilly, she said that if you wanted to be alone tonight she'd sleep in my room and you could have her room. We all want you to be comfortable." Becky told her she'd rather sleep in the room with someone. "Good. We'll bunk in my room. Is there anything else you need to tell me? I know how having trust in someone is hard. You just wait if you have to and tell us what you want."

Becky was overwhelmed by the help she was getting. More so that none of them seemed to care that she was the daughter of a nasty mean man. She hoped her aunt Josephine would be able to help her. She was the only hope she had of never going to live with her father again.

~*~

"Joey, there's a call for you." She turned and looked at the man she'd hired just yesterday to answer calls for her. "He said it's important he speaks with you now."

"Tell him to fuck off." Turning back to the work she was doing, she knew that Harvey, her secretary, wasn't going to last the day if he didn't stop bothering her with little shit. "Well? Did you tell him?"

"No. He said he'd have to have the police come here if you didn't want to hear what he has to say. I'm not sure telling him to fuck off is such a good idea." She stomped toward him. "Don't hurt me."

That stopped her dead in her tracks. She'd never hurt anyone. Joey knew she had a volatile temper, but she never hurt people. Telling Harvey she was sorry for snapping at him, she picked up the phone and gave the idiot who called her today all she wanted to in the way of anger.

"You had fucking better have your ducks in a row, you uneducated couch potato. I'm working, in the event no one told you. What the fuck do you want?" His laughing wasn't something she thought was helping. "I'm hanging up now. If you ever call here again, I will—"

"Your niece, Rebecca Hightower, has been murdered." Joey slid to the floor, her legs suddenly no longer strong enough to hold her up. She asked the man if her husband had done it. "At this point, we're only *assuming* he did. Not that he was the one that pulled the trigger, but I think you understand what might have happened. Her daughter, Becky, is staying with my family. Becky told me I wasn't to trust your sister, Margaret, with any information."

"No. Don't call her. She and Peter are close. I think she is still having an affair with him despite him being married to Rebecca. Where are you?" Ian told her his name as well as where they were. "And Becky? Is she hurt too? It wouldn't be any sweat off his balls to kill his own child."

"She's fine. Scared out of her mind. The doctor told us she was dehydrated and malnourished. We're taking care that she is getting plenty of food and water. Rebecca is tagged as a Jane Doe for now. The police are friends of the family and have taken precautions to make sure no one knows of her death or that she was found. Becky told my daughter that her father would kill us all if he were to find us helping her."

"More than likely, he would. He's not the best of people to be around." Joey thought of all the things she knew about Peter. "I'd like to come and see Becky if you think it'll be safe. I don't want her hurt either. She and Rebecca have been through a great deal while she was married to that fat fuck."

"You certainly have a way with words." She laughed with him. "If you don't mind me saying so, I thought that with you being Becky's great aunt, you'd be — at least sound a little older. You can't be much older than Rebecca was."

"We're all three the same age. Margie and I are twins. Rebecca is my older brother's daughter. He was only sixteen when he got this girl, Sheila, pregnant. Mom had just found out that she was going to have us. It was a race, Mom used to tell us, to see who delivered first. We were born a day earlier than Rebecca. My brother committed suicide about a week after his child was born." Ian told her he was sorry. "Me too. I have no idea why I'm telling you this. You more than likely have a lot of things going on there too. Anyway, I'm not going to be coming there until I hear from you. Also, call me on my cell phone from now on. If you call and I don't answer, it's because I'm working. But I will return your call if you leave me a message."

After giving him the phone number, she told him she wanted to speak to Becky if she could. Ian told her he'd make sure she called her back when he returned home tonight. She was staying with his wife and her sisters.

"Christ, man. How do you live in a house full of women? You must be the most patient person in the world do be able to do that." Ian laughed, and she had to smile. He had a good laugh, one she thought she'd like to hear more often. "Just keep me updated, please. And when the time is right, I'll tell my sister. She's a pain in the ass most of the time, so I won't subject you to that. Also, if you could tell Becky, I love her, that would be great. Thanks for telling me, Ian. I'm sorry you're involved in this. But I do appreciate you taking care of Becky for me. She's the best thing Peter ever did."

After hanging up, she sat there on the floor, wondering what she was supposed to do now. If it were up to her, she'd hire someone to kill Peter off, then live a very happy life behind bars. But she'd made a promise to Rebecca that she'd not kill him or hire anyone to kill him. She'd feared for her life.

"Joey? Am I fired?" She looked up at the Harvey and realized she had to be a nicer person. When a man older than her was afraid of her, then she was most certainly doing shit wrong. She told him she was sorry. "I knew you said no phone calls, but when he told me the police would be involved, I thought it best that he told you instead of the police showing up. That really would have upset you."

"It would have. You did the right thing in that." She told him again she was sorry. "I've been under a great deal of pressure with this work. I don't want to mess it up, and with all the stress of that, I tend to be snappish. I'll work on trying not to make you fear me in the future."

"I thank you for that."

She nodded, then stood up. When he went back to his desk, she went back to her workroom. Being a clothing designer wasn't as glamorous as people saw on television and movies. It was difficult work trying to keep one step ahead of the people in the same industry. Not to mention having an idea what colors would be hot when the next season rolled around. Not that Joey put that much stock in the trends.

Joey designed for the everyday woman. No puffy sleeves for her. Nothing made of taffeta or silk for this line. She did design clothing for evening wear, but her meat and potatoes were the things that women wore every day to work or even for shopping — sturdy clothing that stood up well to time, washing, and the seasons.

"If you were to ask me if I'd wear that color, I'd have to tell you no. What is that called?" She looked over at her best friend and the woman that had given birth to her. Her mom was her partner too. Joey told her mom the color. "Pumpkin pie? You have got to be kidding me. If I had a pie of that color, I'd think it had turned. What are you going to mate it to?"

"Purple." When she picked up the paisley print she'd been searching for before the call came in, she hung it on the board in front of her next to the pumpkin pie. She knew it would work, but she still wanted her mom's opinion. "What do you think? Too much?"

"No. I think it works well. I can see this in a shirt and the pie in a pair of shorts, or even a nice pair of pants. I know you hate the word slacks, but that's what I was thinking of when I saw it. I really do like it." Nodding, she put the two colors on the plate with the design. "I have a feeling you're avoiding telling me about the phone call." Joey nodded but didn't look at her mom. "What is it, baby? Does it have to do with Rebecca?"

"She's gone." Mom nodded but didn't say anything as the two of them spoke quietly. "Becky is all right. Staying with a family in Ohio. I can't go there until they figure out what to do about Peter. I'm also not telling Margie."

"No. She'd be all over that. Crowing to the winds that she is going to be the next Mrs. Hightower. The two of them should have married, to begin with. Then it would have been over with for this family. You know as well as I do that she would have cut ties with us so quickly we'd need a birth certificate to prove she's related to us."

It was nearly nine that night when she heard from Becky. They talked for over an hour, and Joey felt so much better for it. She was being watched and taken care of. Also, she'd turned over the book and all the other things she'd collected in her young life to be put in the family safe. Joey wasn't sure how good of an idea that had been, but there was little she could do about it from here.

After hanging up with her niece, she was ready for bed. But a call from her sister, of all people, kept her up for the rest of the night.

"What happened today at work?" She asked Margie what she was talking about. "You. You got an important phone call that sent you to the floor. What is it? Rebecca again? If you know anything about her, you'd better be telling me, Joey. You know she's run off again with his child."

"How would I know she's run off? And the last time I remembered, Rebecca is a grown woman and can run off without people knowing about her whenever she wants. Are you having me spied on?" Margie said she was. "Why? What could you having me spied on do for you? I run a design shop, Margie. What on earth do you think you're going to find out by doing that?"

"You never know. I did find out you were upset, didn't I? Were you going to call me and tell me about it? Doubtful. When did you become so secretive, Joey? It's not a good look for you." Joey asked her sister when she'd become so paranoid that she had to have her watched. "When you started not taking my side when it came to Peter. He's a good man, you know. You should have more respect for him. All those things the paper is saying about him are lies, and you'd know that if you were to get to know him a little."

"I'm not even sure why you'd think I should care what his life is like. As for what the papers say, your little spy should have told you I don't have a newspaper delivered, nor do I own a television." Margie told her she told her that. "Goodbye, Margie. I don't know where you got your information, but I'm not discussing my personal life with you. Call off your spy, or I will. And press charges."

It was a woman. Joey decided she was going to take measures she'd never thought she'd have to with her own family. Making two phone calls, she felt better for taking a stand. In the morning, only a few hours from now, she was going to do what she should have done long ago, start keeping an eye on those that worked for her. Joey had been slacking on a lot of things of late. Well, no more.

Chapter 12

Pierce decided he'd been gone from home long enough. Getting things set up for Demi had taken less time than he'd thought it would, so he'd put in for some vacation time. It was not only overdue but just what he needed.

Being a cashier for most of his life, from the age of sixteen until Demi came into their lives, had given him a great understanding of people. He could tell, just with a glance, what sort of income they had, if they had children, and what sort of mood they were in. Twice, since working for Demi, as a people person, he'd been able to take what could very well have been a nasty situation and turned it around.

Not even bothering with calling his family to tell them he was finally home, he made his way up to his bedroom and lay down on the bed. Who knew that being on a beach for a week could be so exhausting. Closing his eyes, Pierce let his body drift beyond where he was and settle into a nice comfortable sleep.

Waking up to the smell of pancakes, his favorite, he wondered where the hell he was. Pierce had no staff, and he was sure no one would break into his home to cook for him. Getting up, he took a long hot shower and made his way down to the kitchen. He shouldn't have been surprised to find his mom there flipping pancakes for him.

"You could have told us you were home. I might well have had dinner for you last night." He told her that was exactly why he'd not told anyone. "Well, plan on it tomorrow night. Your father saw your car in the driveway and knew you were home. If you didn't want us to know, you should have parked that thing in the garage. Here, take these. I have things to tell you."

Pierce didn't care for syrup or fruit on or in his pancakes. He would take them, wrap them around his sausage, which his mom had made for him too, and eat them like a hot dog. Mom had finally given up on telling him what a heathen he was about it.

He was finishing off his second pancake bun when she handed him a glass of juice, as well as setting a glass of tea down for herself. He knew it was serious when she squeezed a lemon in her tea, something she only did when she was stressed.

"There is a young girl living with your brother and his new wife. Ian has those two sisters there too. I worry that this, having this girl there, will upset the wonderful life we have now." He asked her what she meant. "She's a cute little thing. Ten years old and loves Cybill. Her mother, who she was with when she died, has been taken to the mortuary under a false name, so her husband doesn't find the little girl."

"Mom, you're only giving me bits and pieces of this, and I'm more confused than I was before I knew anything. Why is her mother dead? And why are we harboring her daughter?" Mom hit him on the forehead. "Mom, you're going to have to start from the beginning and tell me what's gotten you so upset, or I'm going to have to go back to bed to nurse my headache."

She got up and dumped the glass of tea in the sink before bringing him the last of the pancakes and sausage. He was full now, so he played with his food while his mom got whatever was going on in her head into some kind of order. Once she told him everything, he was glad he'd not taken another bite.

"I've spoken to him before. Working for Demi in Illinois. The man would come into one of the stores I was working with and pick up a few things. There were always several men with him, all of them dressed in dark suits and sunglasses. I've never understood that. Why wear something that is going to make you stand out in a crowd?" She asked him if he was nice. "Not particularly. He was mad because we had no lobster tails to go with the steak he wanted for dinner. I had to tell him that while that did sound all right, the store wasn't equipped to have a holding tank for an occasional sale of a lobster. He wanted fresh, you see."

"Did he threaten you or anything?" He told his mom what had happened. "You're kidding me. He offered to pay for a tank to be put in just for him. What were you to do if someone else decided to have a lobster that night? Would you have had to kill them off or something?"

"You've been watching too many of those cop dramas. But he did get more upset when I told him the store wouldn't do it. There just weren't enough sales for it." The store was going to have to close down anyway, he told her. "The town is sort of going downhill. And no matter how many businesses Demi brings in to help the town, they don't seem to want to work."

"That's so sad. Will she lose a lot of money?" Pierce told her she was losing money anyway because very few people could afford to shop at a high-end grocery store like this one. "Why doesn't she lower her cost by putting in a cheaper one? Never mind. I've gotten off track. This man, he's looking for his wife and child. The book I told you about, it's in some kind of code, just like my drama shows, but no one can break it yet."

"Where is the little girl now? Did you mean her when you were telling me about Ian having girls at his home?" She said that was what she meant. "Good. I mean, if anyone could handle having a lot of women around, it would be him."

Mom glared at him, but he kept a straight face while making fun of his brother. Mom brought him up to date on a couple of other things while she browned a roast he'd not had before he left, and put it in the oven to cook. She even put on some green beans — again, something he'd not had before — as she told him about the bakery and the magic that Ian and Lucy now had.

"So they can dress themselves and see a little bit into the future. Those don't sound like too bad of things to have."

Mom told him there were more, but they were only learning about what they had a little at a time. "I'd probably be doing it that way as well. Being overwhelmed isn't good when you don't know what you're going to do if you point a loaded finger at someone."

"What is wrong with you?" Pierce couldn't help it, he laughed. "I'm trying to be serious here, and you're taking potshots at everything I tell you. Have you lost your ever loving mind?"

"Not that I'm aware of. But I did just come back from the nicest vacation I've ever taken. Demi let me use one of her homes while I was working with the stores she had, and it was wonderful to have staff and people waiting on me. But getting to lay on a beach, her own private one, as a matter of fact, made me take a good look at my life. I realized I'm much too serious all the time. I need to take a step back and have some fun. Even if it's something I've done."

"You were terribly serious all the time. The only time I ever saw you happy, it seemed, was when you were cooking. Do you still enjoy that?" He nodded at her. "Good. I just needed to talk to someone, really. I know you'll be updated on the things going on around here, but I'm feeling a little lost lately. Like too much is going on, and I just don't know what to worry about the most. To be honest with you, I'm a little afraid someone from that family is going to be one of my son's mates. Whatever will we do with a mobster in our home?"

"Love them. Try and see what the good is with them. You never know, Mom. They might well hate being with a mobster as much as you do having one in your home." He kissed her on the cheek as he got up to wash up the dishes she'd used. "Are you really having everyone over for dinner tomorrow night? If so, I'm going to bake something. Unless Lucy is going to."

"She is, but only bread, she told me. I've never seen such a neat baker before. She washes up as she goes, like I do, but when she's putting the bread into the pan to rise, there isn't a thing out of place. I think she has little faeries working around her." They both laughed. "You come over around six, and we'll have a nice dinner. Bring the dessert with you, and I'll have a good time knowing that at least one of my sons likes to cook as much as I do."

After his mom left him, he made his way to the living room. It was a room that he spent the most time in, and he was glad for the fireplace. It was only just September, and it was already showing signs of being a hard winter. Not that it mattered to him. He could be in the cold weather all the time.

Unpacking his laptop was the first thing he did. After looking over the reports he'd made on Demi and Lucian's three stores, he sent them off to them. There were also notes he'd taken and sent to them daily, but they had the report now, and he was sure one or both of them would call him about his recommendations on what to do with them.

Almost as if he'd summoned him, Lucian was at his door. "When did you get back?" He told him he'd gotten home last night, and had slept well. "Mom told me she'd been to see you and that you were getting the rod out of your ass. She didn't actually say that, but she did tell us you were trying to be funny. And that she didn't get it."

"She didn't. Stress is what she blamed it on. I think she never gets jokes. Anyway, are you here about the paperwork or just to bust my chops for something?" Lucian told him both. "Oh, good. You know what? I didn't miss that when I was working. I do have a question for you, however. It's nothing big, but when is Demi going to pop that kid? I saw her on video calls, and she looks like she's having fifty kids."

"Don't say that to her, for Christ's sake." When Lucian looked around, he did as well. Pierce wondered if he was worried Demi was going to come out of the woodwork. "She has three more weeks to go. The doc told her she's doing very well, but the baby is going to be big. Mom told her how much I weighed, and that worried her for days. So we don't ask so we don't upset her again. I think she beat a medicine bag to death that day. Anyway, I'm glad you're home."

"Me too. Even with all the drama around here, I'm thrilled to be back." They talked about the paperwork, and Pierce was impressed that Lucian was so up to date on all the things going on with the businesses he shared with Demi. "I'm recommending you close down Shepherds Wake. It's a nice shop, but there aren't enough people around there in the off months to make it worthwhile to even stock lettuce. If you close that one down, I think it will generate more business for the other store in the area."

"Demi told me last week that the store was losing money. Not from stealing this time, but simply because it was difficult to keep it stocked up the few weeks out of the year that people travel there, then to not stock it the other weeks out of the year. She told me she was thinking of changing it to simply an ice cream place." This store was on Martha's Vineyard, a touristy place to go.

"That would work. The two on the boulevard have gone to soft serve. And there isn't another one for about fifty miles. She could make a killing off just having cones. I can see it branching out to a quick burgers and fries kind of place, but specializing in ice cream." Lucian asked him if he meant like that place Mom used to take them as children. "Yes. Youngs Jersey Dairy farm was just what I was thinking about when I thought of the ice cream place. They do a hell of a business year round too. And have special attractions for the kids and adults. Remember playing putt-putt there?"

"Yes. Gosh, I've not thought of that place in years." They talked about some memories they'd made as kids. Most of it, not surprisingly, had to do with doing a lot of free or inexpensive things. They'd been broke but never felt like it. "I'm going to take Mom and Dad there soon. I know they'd enjoy it."

"So would Ian's girls and the rest of the grandchildren." They planned a date to go, and Lucian told him he'd get back to him on it. "Mom is having dinner tomorrow night. It would be a great time to bring it up. I'm sure we can work on a date that everyone can go."

After his brother left, Pierce was feeling tired again. He set his timer for an hour, then lay on the couch. The fireplace was going, and he was nice and warm for the first time in a while. Closing his eyes, he wondered about what his mom had said. What if a mobster's family member became a part of their family?

"We'll deal with it like we do everything else. Loudly and efficiently." That brought a smile to his face, and he realized he didn't care. "It will, or it won't, that's my new mantra."

Before You Go...

HELP AN AUTHOR

write a review

THANK YOU!

Share your voice and help guide other readers to these wonderful books. Even if it's only a line or two, your reviews help readers discover the author's books so they can continue creating stories that you'll love. Log in to your favorite retailer and leave a review. Thank you.

Kathi Barton, a winner of the Pinnacle Book Achievement award as well as a best-selling author on Amazon and All Romance books, lives in Nashport, Ohio, with her husband, Paul. When not creating new worlds and romance, Kathi and her husband enjoy camping and going to auctions. She can also be seen at county fairs with her husband, who is an artist and potter.

Her muse, a cross between Jimmy Stewart and Hugh Jackman, brings her stories to life for her readers in a way that has them coming back time and again for more. Her favorite genre is paranormal romance, with a great deal of spice. You can visit Kathi on line and drop her an email if you'd like. She loves hearing from her fans. aaronskiss@gmail.com.

Follow Kathi on her blog: http://kathisbartonauthor.blogspot.com/

www.ingramcontent.com/pod-product-compliance
Lightning Source LLC
Chambersburg PA
CBHW020620180626
46810CB00007B/2867